A Prayer for the Damned

and Other Tales of the West

For information, contact: henrygraypub2022@gmail.com

Publisher's Cataloging-in-Publication Data:

Names: Cornet, Joe, 1961-.
Title: A prayer for the damned and other tales of the West / Joe Cornet.
Description: Granada Hills, CA : Henry Gray Publishing, 2024. | Includes 10 b&w
    photos.
Identifiers: LCCN 2024916951 | ISBN: 978-1-960415-30-1 (hbk.) |
    ISBN: 978-1-960415-29-5 (pbk.) | ISBN: 978-1-960415-31-8 (ebook)
Subjects: LCSH: Western stories. | Bounty hunters - Fiction. | Clergy - Fiction. |
    Outlaws - Fiction. | New Mexico - History - 19th century - Fiction. | BISAC:
    FICTION / Westerns. | FICTION / Action & Adventure. | FICTION /
    Historical / Civil War Era.
Classification: LCC PS36.3.076 P73 2024 | DDC 813 C—dc23
LC record available at https://lccn.loc.gov/2024916951

Made in the United States of America.

Published by Henry Gray Publishing, P.O. Box 33832,
Granada Hills, California, 91394.

All names, characters, places, events, locales, and incidents in this work are fictitious creations from the author's imagination or used in a fictitious manner. No character in this book is a reflection of a particular person, event, or place. The opinions expressed are those of the characters and should not be confused with the author's.

For more information or to join our mailing list, visit HenryGrayPublishing.com.

A PRAYER FOR THE DAMNED

and Other Tales of the West

JOE CORNET

HENRY GRAY HG PUBLISHING

Granada Hills, CA
"Select books for selective readers"

CONTENTS

CONTENTS

OTHER TALES OF THE WEST

Foreword

by Don Murray

It is my pleasure to introduce Joe Cornet's first book of fiction, *A Prayer for the Damned and Other Tales of the West.*

I have had a long association with the Western film genre and the legacy of the American West, so I have looked forward to reading these Western tales. They are exciting, heroic, and often terrifying. The first story is based on Joe's original screenplay (with some new twists!) from his first Western feature, while the other three are entirely new stories.

I played a role in Joe's film *Promise.* See if you can spot my character in this new book of stories.

Chapter 1

Remembrance

Daylight was ebbing. Mattie sat in her favorite rocking chair on the porch. Harold, the boy who lived next door, had left a box of groceries in the tiny kitchen at the back of the modest house. "Let me know tomorrow if you need anything else, Miss Mattie," he said. "My folks and I will be at church in the morning, but I'll stop in just after the service."

Mattie waved him off and assured the young boy that she was just fine. She had not even yet put the groceries in the pantry. The tea kettle next to her, on a small table, was still warm. She poured another cup. At this hour of the day, the kettle always contained a dram of whiskey, a fact the neighbors would never have suspected for such a kindly woman in her final years.

Most people who knew her had no idea of the life Mattie had led years ago. A young life filled with violence, cruelty, and tears. Yet there was beauty as well, and love. As she sipped the spiked tea, she wondered: had it really been that long ago? Was it real, or was it just a dream? It certainly felt like a dream, hazy and ethereal, but one series of events was indelibly imprinted in her mind – a grand yet terrifying adventure which culminated in an event that would alter the intended course of her life. And so her mind turned back to that terrible and wonderful time.

Chapter 2

Sudden, New Mexico Territory
(Thirteen years after the Civil War)

Nothing ever happened in Sudden. A copper strike in 1852 produced about a dozen tents in the area. When the copper ran out a year later, a small town sprouted up in this spot for no reason. The town expanded again in the early '60s when word spread that a Confederate barracks was to be located nearby. That never happened.

The war came and went without ever affecting this section of the territory. More people arrived for no reason, and they stayed. Still, nothing ever occurred until that one day, thirteen years after Appomattox.

The lone rider approached Sudden around mid-morning. The heat was already oppressive, which was why no one was about in the streets of the town. Only a mute boy drawing water from the public well gave away the fact that people actually lived here. The boy looked into the distance and saw the lone rider as he entered the far end of the main street.

The rider seemed uneasy in the saddle atop a magnificent blue roan at least seventeen hands high. As he rode nearer up the main street, the boy sensed something was wrong. The rider swayed to and fro as if intoxicated, but it was more grave than that.

The boy dropped the bucket down the well and ran to the rider. The face of the rider was clearly in a daze, and as the boy ran behind the horse, he could see blood stains on the rider's back. The horse stalled. The rider wiped the sweat from his brow, and then he fell off his mount, face down, into the dusty street. The boy could not cry out, so he ran into the general store to alert someone.

This was how the town of Sudden was introduced to Cole.

Chapter 3

We Won't Be Needing This Today

A shingle hung in the midsection of a wooden door that read:

DOCTOR JULY HARRIGAN
GENERAL PRACTITIONER, SURGEON

The interior of Dr. Harrigan's office and examination room was cluttered with the tools of his trade. A skeleton suspended from a rack watched over the examination room. The shelves were packed with medical books, journals, specimen jars, and a myriad of bottles containing medicines.

Cole lay face down on an examination bed, the back of his shirt ripped open, and his backside covered in blood. Dr. Harrigan pondered the shot-up mess in front of him. Various trays of medical probes, clamps, forceps, and other tools stood at the ready. Dr. Harrigan chose a particular forceps and used it to extract lead from the patient's various wounds. He did this repeatedly, dropping each lead slug into a metal pan with a tinny thud. He dropped the forceps into the tray to grab a small rag to mop the sweat from his brow, which he then used to mop up the excess blood on Cole's backside.

Dr. July Harrigan picked up a decidedly nasty bone saw and looked at it, as if with a sigh of regret. "Well, I guess we won't be needing this today." He took a beat, then grabbed the forceps yet again to go back to work.

"The situation might have been worse as I was scheduled to go to Tucumcari with my wife and family this morning, but that damn train was delayed again. My fellow medical colleague here in town came down with the diphtheria last week. That would have left you high and dry for any treatment. Fortunately, for you, I am still here due to a failed railway timetable!"

Cole winced at each probe as a beautiful woman with straw-colored hair held his hand tightly.

The doctor dropped another slug into the pan with another tinny thud. "I've been waiting three weeks for the ether to arrive from St. Louis. My sincere apologies for the use of medicinal spirits in lieu of a stronger anesthetic. If you want to scream, go right ahead. The music teacher upstairs is out for a recital this afternoon. Calls to mind when I practiced in a tent in Abilene. In those days, the patient could caterwaul his head off as those streets were noisier than a Chinese laundry."

Dr. Harrigan's fingers fiddled about the tray in front of him, and with a great deal of flourish, he chose another probe. "Yes, sir, I've treated them all. Soldiers, sailors, and now you shootists. I just don't get what motivates you boys. Seems like an awful risk for a net result you fellas usually have to split up with another confederate. Still, it's a living."

Cole rolled his eyes at the woman with the straw-colored hair and continued wincing as the doctor wielded his probe.

"Some of these authors of the penny dreadfuls are trying mighty hard to elevate you boys to some kind of mythic status. Like noble Greek gods dispensing a kind of frontier justice through extreme acts of bravery. Frankly, I just can't see it. Take my grandfather, now there was a true hero. He spent his youth crisscrossing the Cumberland Gap. In those days, the Indians eviscerated the pioneers they caught. Believed that would prevent their souls from entering the spirit world. Yep, that took some real courage and fortitude to face old Chief Dragging Canoe."

Cole had had enough. He started to raise himself upward with his arms and screamed out, "Jesus Christ, Mattie! Can't you tell this son of a bitch to shut up?"

"I think you just did, Cole," Mattie shot back at him.

The doctor pushed him back on the table. "Easy there, fella. You start moving around, and the lead will sink in deeper."

Cole laid back down with a sigh.

"Just makes my job tougher. I can't dig in there much past an inch. That's what the manual says. You got yourself into this condition, now let me do the repair work." Dr. Harrigan paused to choose another instrument. "Like I was saying, Chief Dragging Canoe was a real terror. It's a wonder that any whites survived that Henderson Treaty land. The old chief declared it was to be a dark and bloody ground."

The doctor changed instruments yet again. "My family left Kentucky after all that. Headed further into the West. Texas, to be exact. Now this was before Travis and his boys glorified that old mission. Yep, my family just kept moving. After the Mexicans gave up at Vera Cruz, that was a sign to push farther west. By God, you know I was the first of my family in two generations to see the East Coast again? Went back east to get my medical education. That decision kept me behind the lines after Sumter. After '63, there were so many men sent back for loss of…"

Cole snapped back, "Listen, can we skip the history lesson?"

"Who did this to you?" Dr. Harrigan inquired.

"Ever heard of The Preacher?" Mattie asked.

Dr. Harrigan made a whistle. "Hardly a soul in this territory who has not heard of him. I thought he was a legend, a bogey man, like Prestor John back in medieval times. A religious myth to keep the faithful in line."

Cole shook his head. "Believe me, he exists."

"I first heard of him at a temperance union meeting in Denver. Some fire and brimstone pastor ranted about this preacher smiting the wicked and cleansing the Southwest of sin," recalled Dr. Harrigan.

Mattie nodded, "That's his reputation, Doc."

"Well, he's got his work cut out for him in this den of iniquity." He changed instruments again. "Did you report this to the law?"

Cole shook his head.

"Seems the sooner you lay this in the lap of the sheriff, the better off you'll be. I'll get you patched and send for Sheriff Duncan to take your statement. You sure don't want that Preacher doing this to anyone else, with perhaps more deadly results. Were you tracking this man?"

Cole replied with a weary voice, "No, but we're on the trail for the same thing."

Doc Harrigan scratched his head. "My God! Well, like I said…I can't see what motivates you shootists. Whatever you seek, is it worth the risk of running up against a demon like that?"

"For him, it is, Doc," said Maggie soberly.

Dr. Harrigan shook his head and probed the last wound. Pulling the lead out, it stuck to his forceps so that the good doctor had to shake it off.

"There's a sticky one on my forceps." The lead ball dropped into the pan. "You fellas and your ill-gotten financial pursuits. Seems to me a stable job like a dry goods salesman would be a better life. Fact is, we need a good dry goods man here in Sudden. You might want to entertain that idea for a more reliable career, that is if you two folks would like to settle here. Would be a more Arcadian lifestyle than your current vocation."

The doctor dropped the forceps with a loud clank into the tray and grabbed another rag. "Now then, that should do it. Let's get you closed up. I'll supply you with a bottle, make that half a bottle of laudanum to quell any lingering pain. You folks have any lodging in town? The Byzantium Hotel is quite comfortable. The new owners just took delivery of fifteen new beds to replace the old ticky ones. They even have a faro table in the lobby."

Dr. Harrigan looked over at Mattie. He pointed to a bottle of liquid on the shelf next to her. "Let me see that bottle, little lady." Mattie passed the bottle to Dr. Harrigan. He uncorked it and took a swig. "We're almost done here."

Chapter 4

Sacrifice in the Southwest

It was dusk at the small rancho. The air was cool, and a slight breeze blew across the small valley. The colors of the setting sun had an ominous glow. Inside the rancho, a homesteader couple sat in chairs, gagged and tied with their backs to each other. Across the room, in a small rocking crib, lay their infant. These were the victims of whatever sin The Preacher had judged upon them.

The Preacher was a big man, six feet in height. He wore all black with a knee-length frock coat sporting a cape. His black flat-brimmed hat tilted forward covering his eyes, he held a well-worn Bible in his left hand and began to speak to the homesteader and his wife. These words would be the final earthly sounds that they would hear.

"I have seen the face of God. I have touched the Almighty's robe. He sends me visions and guides me through the corrupted valleys of life. I am the one, the righteous appointee to spread the word and administer justice." The Preacher pulled back the brim of his hat to reveal his eyes. They were hollow and dark. His voice now assumed a louder tone, as if he were at a pulpit. "I shall tame this new land and instill in its people the word and the truth of the holy message. Do you hear me, wicked ones? This territory is an evil limbo. Wickedness walks hand-in-hand with avarice. I am His tool to wipe this land clean of all that is an affront to His name. Confess your sins and embrace my truth."

At this moment, The Preacher reached down with his right hand to draw back the flap covering his cross-draw holster. He drew his '58 Remington. Cocking the gun, he leveled it at the homesteader and then at his wife, and then back and forth, and back and forth again. The Preacher walked over to the cradle and nudged it with the toe of his boot. The cradle rocked back and forth, the infant giggled, and The Preacher walked back to the homesteader and his wife. "Confess your sins and embrace my truth!"

Two shots rang out. The Preacher's boots lumbered across the floorboards, and a third shot rang out. Divine justice had been carried out. Whatever crime or effrontery to God had been invented in The Preacher's twisted and warped mind, justice had been delivered.

Three days later, the bodies were discovered in the little rancho by a ranch hand. No one in this part of the territory ever knew who committed these murders, except for The Preacher.

Chapter 5

Sheriff Duncan Makes a Discovery

Thaddeus Duncan proudly served as the sheriff of Sudden. He was a man of routine, structure, and order. Sheriff Duncan truly lived by everything being in its right place. Coffee, eggs, and bacon at 8 AM every morning. His dutiful rounds of Sudden at 4 p.m. every day. Church each and every Sunday. Steak and beans for dinner every Friday night at Ma Bailey's Cafe. Turned into bed by 9 PM every night.

In the hillsides above the town of Sudden, he rode his longtime faithful horse Buck, a quarter horse he had owned for more than a decade. As they moved up the narrow trail together, Sheriff Duncan did what he always did – he spoke to Buck. Even though Buck couldn't reply, the Sheriff had many great conversations with him. "Well, Buck, I got as much information as I could out of that manhunter. Even though he was fairly shot to pieces, he was pretty cold, focused, and reticent. It's as if he didn't want to tell me one damned thing. I told him, Buck, that I was the law around here, and any danger that threatens this town is my responsibility. Still, it was everything I could do to get even this scrap of information out of him as to where he was ambushed. Maybe he was just showing off for the sake of that pretty girl who was shuffling playing cards all the while we talked."

Just then, a dust devil spun up, blowing sand into Sheriff Duncan's eyes. Buck reared up. Sheriff Duncan grabbed his reins, and Buck settled down. The sheriff wiped his eyes. His vision was slightly out of focus, but as it cleared, he found himself and Buck among sharp, jagged rocks jutting out of the ground. A wind started to whip up, which sounded almost like a howl or a plaintive wail. They moved together much more slowly now. Sheriff Duncan dismounted, grabbed Buck's reins, and then the two began walking together. The wailing wind continued, and Sheriff Duncan looked up at the darkening sky. He felt a mysterious chill in his bones. "You know, Buck, I have a strange feeling like I am entering someplace haunted."

A few yards down, they came upon a clearing. Sheriff Duncan looked down and noticed dried bloodstains on the ground. "Well, Buck, this must have been where it happened. Just look at all the blood."

The two compadres moved towards a mound of piled-up rocks. Sheriff Duncan dropped Buck's rein, he wasn't going anywhere. Duncan moved up to the strange rock structure. It almost resembled some kind of primitive church pulpit. "Looks like an opportune place to ambush someone from. Well, look at this, Buck. Look at this…"

Sheriff Duncan grabbed a piece of paper that had been affixed to a Joshua tree. "It looks like... a page out of a Bible, this verse is circled right here, but it's got some words crossed out. Ha! Now who in the hell thinks they can edit the Bible?" Sheriff Duncan read to Buck from the paper, "For I am God's servant, if you do wrong, be afraid. I do not bear the sword in vain. I am the servant of God, an avenger who carries out God's wrath. Revelation 21:8."

Sheriff Duncan took his hat off his head and mopped his brow. "Someone's trying real hard to take over the good Lord's job. Now last time I checked, the good book says, 'Vengeance is mine, sayeth the Lord.'"

The sheriff put his hat back on his head and walked around the rock pulpit, kicking the dirt with his boot. He spied a couple half-smoked cigars and picked them up. "Boy howdy. What do we have here?" Duncan smelled one of the cigar stubs and threw it back down to the ground. "If that don't beat all, Buck, I don't recognize the smell. This cigar ain't from nowheres around these parts. I don't like this, Buck. You know who this looks like? I don't like this one bit. Let's get back to town, amigo."

Sheriff Duncan folded the manuscript and stuck it into his vest pocket. All the way back down the hill, the wind continued its wailing, and the sky drew ever darker.

Chapter 6

I'll Forget You Just Said That

The Darkwood Saloon and Gambling Hall was without a doubt the most vile and dangerous establishment in the town of Sudden. Even the dedicated Sheriff Duncan would never step foot in this place without at least one deputy and a Henry rifle for backup. The Darkwood had first opened during another false copper strike in the hills above Sudden. The vein ran out quickly, but the saloon stayed, much to the disgust of some of the good Christian folks in the town. If anyone ever wanted to get himself shot to pieces, this was a good place to find the bullets.

The owner was a disreputable sort named Lamar. Nobody ever really knew his last name, but that didn't matter since Lamar was missing his left ear, so everyone knew who he was anyway. Some reports say that Lamar only served the rotgut whiskey that Comancheros sold to the tribes. No one who set foot in the Darkwood cared about this, because the only purpose of setting foot in the bar was to play a serious, big-time game of poker. Over the years, thousands of dollars changed hands, and dozens of men were shot up, knifed, or garroted within the confines of the smoke-filled rooms. All the while, Lamar laughed all the way to the bank as he sold his rotgut whiskey at double the price of the real aged-in-a-keg juice. From time to time, he took a piece of the action from some of the bigger games.

On one side of the saloon were all the gaming tables. On the other side of the saloon was a piano that had never been in tune. Above the piano, where there should have been a painting of a pretty lady in a stage of undress, there was a dark oil painting of a succubus.

As the pale, sickly piano player banged out the tune "Red Wing," Mattie sat across the room at a table with three men. All the players had folded, and Mattie drew the winning hand and was collecting the coins from the center of the table. Cigar smoke was everywhere.

A mountain of a man with a full white beard and a German accent said to anyone within earshot, "Well, that plays me out."

An astute man, much younger, responded to him, "You out, Charlie?"

"Too rich for me. Lady, I'm out," said the mountain of a man with the German accent.

Mattie tipped the brim of her hat to this gentleman and said, in a soft but respectful voice, "I admire your skill."

The German player got up from the table. "Too good for me. You coming, Emmett?"

His partner turned to him. "I guess. See you, ma'am."

Both men doffed their hats, turned, and walked out of the bar. There was a long silence as Mattie counted up her winnings.

The third man, finely dressed and well-groomed, turned to Mattie. He was obviously drunk. "Well, I guess that just leaves the two of us, honey."

Mattie stopped counting the coins. "My name is Mattie. Don't call me honey."

"After all the money you've been hogging for the last hour, I figure I can address you anyway I want," declared the man.

"What's that supposed to mean?" asked Mattie.

The unctuous man leaned in and, in a low voice, said, "Don't think your tricks have escaped me."

"What in the name of God are you talking about?"

"No way a little filly like you could clean us all out the way you did just on your own. You using marks? Mirrors, maybe?"

Mattie leaned back in her chair and tried not to regard this man with any degree of seriousness. "I'll forget you just said that."

The man laughed. "Hear talk over in Santa Fe about a woman card cheat. You be her?"

"Again, I will forget you said that."

The man turned livid and righteous. "I ain't no tin horn, lady! I was an Indian affairs agent for ten years, so I know a thing or two about cheating."

Mattie could feel the disgust rising within her. She put on a wry smile and said, "So you know how to cheat the red man?"

The drunk man turned loud. "I was referring to the devious cheating they did on us! I seen it all!"

"Listen, what the hell are you driving at?" asked Mattie.

The man scratched at his long, walrus-like mustache. "I think you give me back my last three hands. That's what I'm driving at."

Mattie steadied herself. She had been in situations like this before, but today she was not in a reliable environment. She was on her own. "Those other two gentlemen didn't seem to object."

"I don't give a two penny damn what those other fellas did. I know when I've been cheated," the man said.

A long silence engulfed the entire room. Lamar looked on with a smile on his face.

Mattie needed a plan. "You can just walk away, Mister."

"Why you little bitch! How about I get the Sheriff?"

"Be my guest. I hear he's a fair-minded man," replied Mattie.

The drunk man shot upright. His chair fell backwards behind him. He leaned in and clenched hold of Mattie's arm. As he loomed over her, she could smell the rotgut whiskey Lamar had been pouring. He stared into her eyes. "You know, lady, we can settle this a different way."

"Nothing to settle. Except your drunkenness," Mattie replied.

The man gripped Mattie's arm harder and started looking up and down at her body. "You ain't much for a figure, but you got a pretty face. I could ignore you're just skin and bones."

Mattie was serious now. "Take your damn hands off me!"

"Don't worry. You won't think it's so bad once you get into it. I ain't never had no complaints."

Mattie's demeanor changed. Her face turned almost seductive. "You some kind of a tiger, huh?"

"A regular beast," the drunk man chuckled.

Mattie responded in a soft voice, "Well, well." The former Indian affairs jasper was too drunk to know what was coming. Mattie grabbed his crotch hard and twisted, she rose up and pulled her knee up into his gut, and just before he fell back, she laid a full right hook directly on his jaw.

The pathetic bastard fell across the table and cracked one of the legs. The table went askew, and bottles and cups went flying.

Nobody responded or reacted, as Mattie just stood there in the Darkwood alone. "I can't abide a man who underestimates me."

Chapter 7

The Mouth of Madness

The Preacher held a firm seat on his McClellan saddle. His horse was black as night. The daylight, however, bore down with intense heat. The eastern end of the Arizona/New Mexico territory could easily resemble one of the circles of hell, except there were no tortured sinners serving an eternity of damnation. Finding sinners and administering the appropriate justice was The Preacher's calling. Over the years, he had sentenced many a transgressor to damnation. He, alone in this territory, had been granted this power.

The Preacher knew all forms of sin. He had witnessed the frail human spirit at its most vile from a young age. Now in his fourth decade of mortality, he had given his life to cleansing this vast spiritual wilderness of all its sin and wickedness. He had made good on his commitment, as a trail of death followed his journey. His reputation and legend were becoming well known and often discussed with fear in many religious circles. That was just fine with him. Was not the hand of God feared in the Old Testament? The Preacher had no sympathy for the compassionate New Testament. "Smite the wicked" was his philosophy. There should be no room for leniency or compassion. The mission remained clear, pristine, and precise – to cleanse sin!

As The Preacher rode on, he mopped his upper lip with a lace handkerchief. The circumstances of the acquisition of this handkerchief were less than pleasant, mostly bloody. Nevertheless, all in a day's work on his endless slog combating sin, greed, and avarice.

A blast from a powerful ray of sunlight hit The Preacher directly in the eyes. He blinked, then slowed his horse, jerking the reins back violently. He felt a sense of dizziness, as if he would faint. This would not do. The Preacher must maintain his fortitude. He mopped his brow with the lace handkerchief again and again. "Be strong, resist, you are the warrior of the Almighty on this earth," he thought. He could not succumb to weakness.

On this note, The Preacher dug his huge Spanish spurs into the belly of his horse, where there were already so many spur wounds. It took off in a canter for another quarter of a mile. The black horse was now foaming white with sweat. The Preacher knew the horse was only a tool. If it collapsed from exhaustion, he would just steal a new mount, even if it meant shooting the owner in the back. God had elevated him above the laws of men.

Once again, a blinding ray of intense sunlight hit him. Jutting his legs forward and pulling the split reins back tight, his horse stopped cold, burrowing its hoofs into the loose sand. The Preacher felt uneasy and then faint again. He either fell or slid off the saddle, he was unsure of which. Drawing to his knees, he looked up at the bright firmament and removed his flat-brimmed hat. It was soaked in sweat. He saw the vision...

A young boy, awkward and scared, running to him. The boy was crying, and suddenly there appeared a dark woman in a gray dress, running to the boy and extending her hand. The boy turned, and the woman disappeared. Suddenly, there appeared an open casket in which lay the woman in the gray dress. Mourners filed by paying last respects. The little boy followed at the end of the line, as a gruff man with a long white beard pushed him along the casket.

The boy was The Preacher.

Chapter 8

Sheriff Duncan Needs Some Information

Buck carried Sheriff Duncan onto the main street of Sudden. The shock and the terror remained in the Sheriff's mind. He pulled Buck up to the hitching post in front of the Sheriff's Office, hopped off the saddle, and tied him to the rail. He took a long look down the main street. Only a few citizens were about doing their daily errands or chores. The calm he sensed contrasted with the feeling of impending doom that he felt. He noticed Dr. July Harrigan walking with purpose towards the White Elephant Saloon. Sheriff Duncan hollered at the top of his voice, "Hey Doc! Doc Harrigan, hold up there!"

The good doctor looked around and saw Sheriff Duncan coming towards him. "Sheriff Duncan, I hear a sense of urgency in your voice. I see a look of puzzlement in your countenance. Something akin to the proverbial foreboding aura of impending doom."

Sheriff Duncan cut him off. "Yeah, yeah, Doc. Listen, I need some information and maybe your opinion."

"I shall endeavor to serve our town constable as best I can."

Sheriff Duncan pulled his hat off and fanned himself. "Let's get out of the sun." They stepped under the awning of the saloon and the Sheriff continued. "How's your patient doing? Healing up okay? Is he going to pull through?"

Dr. Harrigan rubbed his chin. "I should say so. He is, indeed, a very determined sort of fellow. I've never seen a patient make such a startling, miraculous, rebounding recovery. Well, that is, at least one of my patients. I expect he'll be up and about soon enough. Of course, his young lady friend is quite a rejuvenating tonic as well."

"Well, good for him. I admire a fighter. But now, Doc, what do we know about this fella? I assume you're checking in on him regular. He said any more about what he's up to? How he got bushwhacked? Where he's headed next?"

The doctor replied, "Nope. Nothing other than what he said under distress the other night. He's a pretty quiet sort as shootists go. Like I told you, he confessed he encountered The Preacher and both he and his lady agree he's lucky to be alive. He's obviously a bounty killer, but there's a sense of honor about him."

Sheriff Duncan leaned in, "Well, I didn't put too much stock in his claims. That was a pretty fanciful story he told you. We both know how many false Preacher fairy tales we've heard over the years, so I decided to check it out. Went up to where he claimed the bushwhacking occurred and you know what? I think he's telling the truth. Just take a gander at this." Sheriff Duncan handed Doc Harrigan the marked-up and edited page of the Bible.

Doc Harrigan read through the page and let out a small whistle.

The Sheriff added, "With those crossed-out words and strange additions, it looks like a pretty distorted version of scripture. Found these, too." He handed over the two half-smoked cigars. "You ever smelled a cigar like that from around here?"

"Can't say that I have," Doc replied. "This all adds up to what I was saying when you walked up. This is very foreboding. Isn't it, Thad?"

The Sheriff took a pause and thought about it. "Fraid so, Doc. Fraid so. This time it's for real. Now we don't want to panic folks, but Doc, you and I have got to be ready for anything. If only a fraction of those Preacher stories are true, we may be in for some dark days ahead."

"Indeed, yes. Indeed so," agreed Doc. "Now this just came to my mind, Sheriff. Might you be thinking of exterminating that scripture twisting vermin yourself and collecting a handsome bounty?"

The Sheriff chuckled. "Dr. July Harrigan, you sure ought to know me better than that. I'm a little too old and a little too comfortable, and I'm no bounty hunter. I'm guessing that Preacher left these clues hoping I'll leave town searching for him. So that is exactly what I'm not going to do."

"Why Sheriff Thaddeus Duncan, I do know you better than that. But I figured I asked in case any of our citizens start getting curious about it.

Say, how about a refreshing libation to keep your spirit up? Step into the saloon. I'm buying."

"Thanks, Doc, but not right now. Gotta telegraph a marshal friend of mine and I'm gonna want to talk to that shootist buddy of yours whenever he's healed up enough. I'll talk to you later." Sheriff Duncan stepped off the sidewalk, crossed the street and headed for the telegraph office.

Doc Harrigan turned and walked into the saloon.

Chapter 9

Cole on the Mend

Up in room 3 on the second floor of the Byzantium Hotel, Cole sat upright in bed. Dr. Harrigan certainly was right – the bed was brand new with no ticks. He was wrapped in bandages covering his torso. He looked across the room and watched Mattie brush her long straw-colored hair. She wore only scant undergarments, which Cole could not help but appreciate. A pitcher of water and a cup was placed at the end table next to the bed. Cole reached for the pitcher and the cup, and started to pour the water when the pitcher slipped from his hand and started to spill water across the bed. "Goddamn it!"

Mattie turned as Cole put down the pitcher. "I can't leave you alone." Mattie got up from the chair, walked across the room, grabbed the pitcher and filled the cup.

Cole took a big swig of the water. She picked up a small cloth and soaked in it the water basin, and then began to wipe his brow and his face. The feeling was refreshing to him. Cole turned to Mattie, "Well, the good news is the pain is subsiding. Hardly touched the laudanum today."

Mattie waited a moment and then said disapprovingly, "They say that stuff is habit forming."

"Don't worry. I've already got enough bad habits. I can't afford one more," Cole responded. "Besides, you remain my primary obsession." He extended his left hand and ran his fingers down the side of her neck and across her mostly bare shoulder.

She looked down at him longingly and smiled. "That's the way I like it."

Cole grabbed the cup of water again and took another large swig, "The boy who brought up my meal said there was some trouble in the Darkwood yesterday. You okay?"

Mattie tucked her hands at her waist. "You know me, I can take care of myself."

Cole did know it. Mattie was a very independent and self-reliant indi-vidual plucky enough to take on anyone or anything. She sure as hell had helped him out of a few scrapes. Cole pulled back the curtain above the bed and looked out the window. "I keep seeing that local sheriff out the window. Almost as if he was looking up here at us."

"Well, you're news in this town."

"Why? Isn't it an everyday occurrence getting back-shot by a deranged man of God?"

Mattie became sullen. She turned to the window. She said nothing.

Cole looked back at her and wondered what was wrong, "Mattie..."

She didn't respond.

He addressed her again, but softer. "Mattie, Mattie..."

She turned back to him and came out of her daze. "I'm sorry, what?"

Cole sensed what was wrong. "Mattie, please be assured I appreciate everything, and I mean everything, you do."

"What makes you think I don't know that, silly?" She moved towards him and Cole looked into her eyes.

"You're good to me," he said.

She sat down on the edge of the bed and leaned into him, stroked his shoulders and put her fingers under the bandages. They kissed passion-ately for several minutes. Mattie pulled up from him and looked straight into his eyes, "It's been over a week. I'm going crazy not having you."

Cole smiled and said, "Well, we can't have you going crazy." They kissed again.

"I'm not asking too much in your condition, am I? What would that doctor say?"

"I'm not interested in finding out," Cole said. "Just take it easier than usual."

"Oh, you bet, honey," Mattie whispered. She rolled on top of him and his backside hit the headboard. He winced with pain. She rolled over across from him and said, "Was that too rough?"

He laughed and took hold of her hand. "I remember as a little boy my mother promised me I would one day meet an angel. An angel with long golden hair."

Mattie waited for a minute. "Yeah? And then what happened?"

"Then you appeared."

They kissed again and Mattie did take it easier than usual.

Chapter 10

Judgment Upon the Wicked

Pearl's Den sat at the edge of one of the largest townships in the eastern territory. Pearl Duvall operated her establishment with the full consent of the local mayor and various county magistrates. In fact, they were some of her best customers. Her establishment was one of the finest sporting houses in the county. Certainly one of the most lucrative.

Inside the Den, Pearl sat at the bar entering numbers into a ledger book. A hot wind and a cloud of dust rolled through the two swinging doors of the entryway. Then the doors burst open and a flash of light from the midday sun beamed in, illuminating the velvet wallpaper, the crystal chandelier, the oriental carpets, and all the other extravagant palatial appointments which made this particular house a true destination for pleasure-seekers.

The Preacher, however, did not seek pleasure. He was after something else entirely.

Pearl turned to the swinging doors and rose up off the bar stool to greet this strange character clad in all black. The Preacher doffed his hat and laid on every bit of Southern hospitality to this madam. "Good day, my dear lady. Would you be the proprietor of this august establishment?"

Pearl stuck out her right hand. "Pearl Duvall, at your service, kind sir. With what needs can I assist you?"

The Preacher bowed and kissed Pearl's hand, and put his hat back on and gave it a tap. He looked directly at Pearl, "Duvall? Duvall... hmm. Would that be any kin to the Duvalls of the Vermilion Parish?"

Pearl looked puzzled. "That county is in Louisiana. My background is from the northeast."

The Preacher's eyes bored into Pearl, almost as if to her soul. He then shot a glance around the room, staring at its opulence, its wealth, and its effrontery to God. The Preacher shook his head, "Ah, no matter. I hold no grudge for the northern side of the Mason Dixon. Tell me, how many pretty young flowers do you have in this colorful den?"

Pearl smiled. "Mister, we got every size, color, and creed."

"May I view the inventory?"

"Certainly." Pearl shouted, "Girls!"

Six young ladies entered the room and lined up side-to-side. There were two dark-skinned damsels with curly hair, two petite pale-skinned girls, a curvy Latina with silky dark hair, and one full-figured missy with ruby red lips. They were all just as advertised. Every size, color, and creed.

The Preacher smiled, but it was not a warm smile. "My goodness. They're all quite fetching. Fetching queens, every one of them."

The Preacher turned back to face Pearl as she asked him, "So, tell me, what piques your gentleman-from-the-South sensibilities?"

As Pearl spoke, The Preacher's head began to throb with pain. At that moment, he saw the truth. In his mind he could see her for what she truly was. He could see the scales on her now widening face and her exposed skin, her fingers elongating and turning into huge claws, and her mouth becoming wider with a protruding split tongue flapping back and forth. He turned to the other prostitutes and saw them for what they were, too. More scaly creatures, daughters of the devil, hooves where their hands once were. He had sensed he would find evil here, and it stood before him awaiting his justice.

The Preacher looked down and spoke unto the creatures, "Madam, when I look at these precious flowers I'm reminded of the sin and ugliness affecting the world. We live in uncertain times when not everything is as it appears. What may be pure or holy to one may just be sloth or evil to another. 'Suffering wrong as the wages of doing wrong. They counted a pleasure to revel in the daytime. They are stains and blemishes reveling in their deceptions,' so spoke Peter The Rock, Madam."

Pearl appeared confused and somewhat shaken. Some of the girls began feeling scared. Pearl thought it a good idea to stand up to this lunatic. "Listen, honey, my girls are all God-fearing Christians. What is all this half-ass biblical tripe?"

The Preacher shouted, "I am the word and the light!"

"Maybe so, honey. But here the word and the light is between these girls' legs. Now what is it going to be before I kick your deranged ass out of here?" shouted Pearl defiantly.

The Preacher spoke in a soft tone. He was clearly frustrated. "You are not listening to the word. My purpose is to cleanse this land from carnality, among many other depravities. "

Pearl Duvall had had just enough. "I shall ask you to leave, sir."

Like lighting The Preacher pulled his Remington on the Madam and the girls. "And as part of my cleansing of this land, I ask for you to deliver all cash and coin immediately."

Pearl stepped back, "What the hell?"

The Preacher kept his low tone, "This action may be confused with that of highway robbery. In truth, it is my holy duty to relieve you and your batch of whores of this tainted money."

The Preacher raised his six gun to the ceiling, cocked the hammer back, and fired a shot. The girls jumped as particles from the ceiling board fell on The Preacher.

Pearl knew what she had to do. "Do what he says, girls." Pearl shot an angry look at The Preacher. "You will not get far with this, you bastard. I have high-placed friends in this county."

The Preacher fired yet another shot into the ceiling and then shouted, "Madam, shut the hell up and get that box!"

Pearl ran behind the bar and clasped the strong box. It was stuffed to the brim, as it had been a good week at the house. She handed the box to The Preacher.

The Preacher grabbed it greedily, tucking it under his arm. He nodded with approval. "There's a good little lamb." He walked over to the ladies in the lineup. "Now, harlots, cleanse your souls and hand over everything to God's representative on earth."

The Preacher then systematically robbed each girl of the money they had tucked into their corsets. He holstered his Remington and then produced a small Colt pocket revolver, with which he shot two girls directly in their temples. The other four screamed. Three ladies ran toward the front door, but he effortlessly shot them all down. The full-figured missy stood still, completely frozen with fear. The Preacher shot her point blank between the eyes. She dropped dead on the floor.

Pearl cringed with fear and screamed. She reached into her bustier, trying to pull out a hidden derringer, but he easily knocked it out of her hand. The gun rattled across the floor.

Then The Preacher tucked the spent pocket pistol back into his waistband. "Madam, I told you once to shut the hell up." He grabbed for his Remington again, which still had four live cartridges, and he proceeded to send Pearl Duvall to hell.

The Preacher stumbled out of Pearl's House in a daze. He knew not where he was nor what he had just done. It was as if he was walking through a horrible dream. Reflexively, he removed the cylinder from the Remington, emptied the spent cartridges and reloaded. It pays to be prepared for the next confrontation, he thought.

It was then that the vision appeared before him. There stood his father, dressed in black, sporting a long cape and holding a bullwhip. The grim visage spoke but in an indecipherable language.

"Damn your tarnished soul to Hell" shouted The Preacher. He fired the Remington at the vision of his father. It always pays to reload.

In an instant, his father disappeared and he stood alone in the street of a town of which he knew not the name. Back to business, he thought, back to the quest and to make his witness before the wicked. The money appropriated from Pearl and her girls would stake him for some time.

Chapter 11

Revelation

Sometime in the year 1863, a dazed, wounded Confederate soldier of unknown rank wandered into the Louisiana town of Labadieville. His rank was unknown as he was devoid of his tunic, which would bear rank, and he wore only his CSA issued boots, trousers and his one piece undergarment. He claimed that he had been walking for days but knew not from where. He did not know his own name nor where he hailed from; whatever regiment this man served was also unknown.

After several days of wandering the streets, some local residents thought he should be cared for by the local lunatic asylum outside of town. The soldier complied in a docile manner.

Once inside the St. Michel Home for the Insane, he was cleaned up, fed and examined by the only doctor in residence, the war having enlisted most all practicing physicians in the South. It was determined or assumed this man suffered a head injury during skirmishes north of the Louisiana state line, probably Mississippi. As the man never spoke it was all conjecture, of course.

So, he sat in his small room for days on end staring out the window. He barely ate. Many treatments were administered, submerging him in water, manacles, hanging him upside down, but none broke his outer shell. Then one day, the doctor decided to put him in the large dining room so he could interact with the other lunatics. At first all he did was stare at a metal cross hanging on the wall. The cross had been a full crucifix until one if the lunatics chewed off the Jesus figurine.

Every Sunday, a catholic priest visited St. Michel. He addressed the residents in the dining hall as there was no chapel. This was how the breakthrough occurred. While listening to that priest, a transformation began taking place in the mind of the former Confederate soldier of un-known rank. Every Sunday, he listened more intently while always staring at the cross on the wall.

Then one Sunday it happened. "I have seen the truth!"

The doctor and the other lunatics turned to the formerly silent sol-dier. Had he really spoken?

From that day forward the soldier spoke frequently to all his fellow inmates. He requested a bible and read in it for hours every day. In the dining hall, he would read aloud from his bible. Some of the more learned lunatics recognized that the soldier's reading of the scripture did not quite match the actual passages. In fact, some readings were distinctly pervert-ed in strange ways. When one of his fellow inmates pointed this out, the former Confederate beat him within an inch of his life for this effrontery. He was then locked in his room for several months.

⸻ ❧❧❧ ⸻

Mattie was wearing an Oriental robe, and sat on the bed looking over at Cole. Something had been gnawing at her. It was this whole business with The Preacher. She knew that Cole was a formidable opponent for just about any hard case he would meet. This Preacher fellow frightened Mattie. There had been close calls before and Mattie had always cleaned Cole's wounds and healed him back to health. But this last run-in seemed in her mind to be the worst one. Mattie grabbed a brush on the night table and reflexively started brushing her long hair. The silence in the room, other than the scraping sound of the straight razor hitting Cole's whiskers, was deafening.

"You know something, honey?" she asked. Cole paused and looked over at her. She continued, "I want you to give this up. It's no good. It's just too damned dangerous."

Cole returned to his razor and said nothing.

"Please, Cole. Please."

Cole wiped the straight edge off and tossed it into the shaving bowl. "We've been through all of this."

"I know. There is just something different about this. I sense evil in all of it."

Cole wiped his face off again with the rag and threw it on the table. He turned completely to her while staying in his chair. "Look, Mattie,

I've been through worse predicaments than this. Remember Bushwhacker Anderson?"

Mattie sure as hell remembered Bushwhacker Anderson. "The last of the Quantrill renegades. I also remember treating that knife wound for six weeks after you caught him."

"I never said it was easy," said Cole. "Besides, we are still living off that federal reward money. This business with that strongbox will put us in tall cotton for years to come."

Mattie dropped the hairbrush on the bed, rose up and walked towards him. Cole grabbed her by the waist and pulled her close. Mattie looked down, picked up the rag and wiped more of the soap off Cole's face. She said, "There are other things we can do. Things we could do to make a living."

Cole rose up into her arms and took a moment. Looking down, he thought pensively and responded to her, "Well, maybe I should take that dry goods salesman job."

Mattie started laughing.

"What the hell is so funny?"

A smile on her face, Mattie looked up at him, driving her fingers into his chest, and said, "I'm just picturing you in a clerk's apron sorting through a shipment of bustles."

"Well, I wasn't serious about it, Mattie." He turned his look back towards the mirror and backed off slightly.

Mattie moved closer to him and put her hands on the collar of his open shirt. She pulled it back and traced her index finger across one scar after another, and said, "I remember the story of this one, and this one, and this one, and this one." All the while tracing over his chest and arms, she added, "Sometimes when you go away I worry so much I can't stand it. What if one day you don't return?" Mattie let go of him and walked over to the bed. She fell onto it, gazing up at the ceiling.

Cole thought about it for a moment, and he knew he had to say something. "I always come back."

Mattie's Oriental robe had been flung open when she fell upon the bed, unashamed of her nakedness. Looking up at the ceiling, she exclaimed, "You said this would be the last time. The last time. If it isn't, I can't go along with you like this. I will not abide the waiting anymore."

Cole approached the other side of the bed and snatched a bottle of whiskey, and he leaned directly over her. What he said, he meant with all his heart: "My solemn promise this will be the last time." He raised his right hand in front of her and held the whiskey bottle in his left hand.

Mattie looked up at him and stared directly into his eyes for a good long time. "It better be, you son of a bitch. Don't leave me alone to a future of dealing cards on a riverboat."

She pulled him to her forcefully. This time, Mattie did not take it easier than usual.

Chapter 12

Ill Wind

The next morning Cole got up bright and early, went downstairs, and had steak and coffee for breakfast. Now that he was finally up and around, today would be the day that he gathered his supplies for the trail. He had much of the information needed to track this thing down, but he didn't have it all. Still, he knew where to look. His quest was to find something that was only thought to be a legend, but Cole knew it was real and he felt certain that his and Mattie's future would be blessed when he obtained this thing. As he left the lobby of the Byzantium Hotel, his boots hit the wooden planks of the sidewalk. As he walked, the planks creaked and groaned along with the clanging sounds of his spurs.

There was a fierce wind about. Dust and debris was swirling in the street, and items such as fabric, papers, and clothing seemed to be caught up in this wind. It made an unnatural howl and the sunlight was obscured, casting an eerie glow. On his way to the general store, he passed the Sheriff's office and overheard the voice of Sheriff Duncan shouting to him from the doorway. Cole had already picked up a few items for the trip and was carrying them over his shoulder.

"Morning, Slim. Looks like you're packing up for a ride."

Cole stopped and turned, and looked over at the doorway, as the wind whipped up more fiercely. "Indeed. I don't believe I've had the pleasure."

Sheriff Duncan was carrying a Henry rifle in his left hand and he motioned with his right to come inside. "Let's get in out of this dust and wind."

Cole reluctantly followed the sheriff, all the while thinking this was rather an inconvenience, what with all the responsibilities he had for a busy day.

The Sheriff racked the Henry onto a mount on the wall. He turned around to face Cole directly for the first time. "You were fairly delirious last time we talked. My name is Duncan. Long time sheriff of this fine community. I'd say you'd be that gentleman who was on that interesting quest."

Cole felt annoyed. "Now what might that be, Sheriff?"

The Sheriff sighed and responded, "Some say it's your own holy grail."

Cole was now truly annoyed at this intrusion into his personal business. "And I'd say that would be a bit dramatic."

Sheriff Duncan shook his head and tried to be more serious. "And I'd add it could be your undoing."

"What is this about, Sheriff?"

Sheriff Duncan looked down and started fiddling with the jail cell keys on this desk. "Over the years I've seen many folks come and go. Their hopes and dreams dashed by the beguilement of the quick fortune."

"Well, what the hell does this have to do with me?"

Sheriff Duncan looked directly at him. "Well, you're that fellow with the young card-playing woman been here in town getting healed up."

"And if that is true?"

"Word is you're after some mythic strongbox dating to the late war between the states."

Cole pondered how this Sheriff could have obtained that information. "And if that is true?"

"Been a slew of fellows looking for that damn box since '66. What entitles you to the contents?" asked Sheriff Duncan derisively.

"Listen, peace officer, have I broken any laws during our stay here? Are there any warrants or handbills on me? Have I done anything?"

Sheriff Duncan smiled. "No, sir. Hear tell you're a right solid character. My concern is for your safety."

Cole was unused to people being concerned about his safety. "How so?"

"You ran into some trouble recently, hence you're stay in our town."

"Well, I, uh…"

Sheriff Duncan quickly interjected, "The Preacher, right? It was The Preacher."

Cole nodded, much as if he had been trying to hide something.

"Oh yes, The Preacher. So many stories about him, it's hard to tell fact from fiction. Some don't even believe he exists. Word is he was a slave catcher in Mississippi before the war. And I'll bet you didn't know that."

Cole shook his head, "I did not."

Sheriff Duncan continued, "And during the war something happened which caused his mind to slip. Spent much of the war in a lunatic house down in Labadieville. Until a bunch of drunk Union soldier boys let loose all the inmates just for the hell of it. Why'd they do that, I have no idea."

Cole had to find a way to leave this office. "You remind me of your local sawbones. Does everyone in this goddamn town like to give a history lesson when speaking?"

Sheriff Duncan threw the keys onto his desk. "This is a dangerous man. He's a special kind of crazy. Thinks he was put on this earth to smite the wickedness out of the West. Hell, even Bill Hickok couldn't achieve that. Got news on the telegraph, there was a posse of marshals and Pinkertons after him. They got close, but he bushwhacked three of them. And you know what he did? Hung their carcasses from a white bark maple outside of Lubbock."

After some pause, Cole looked back at the Sheriff. "Believe me, I know the bastard's dangerous."

"This Preacher fellow is after that damn box, too. Story is the fortune inside will build up his weird place of worship where he can preach his invective. Well, I say we have enough sheep dip in the territory without that son of a bitch." He looked at Cole. "I hear you have a good lady."

"The finest."

"Then what do you want with this terrible matter?"

"I've seen worse."

"Mister, I've buried too many of you fortune hunters over the years. Take my advice – go back to the Byzantium Hotel. Cherish your woman, revel in life, get yourself a steak dinner and forget this bad business."

Cole thought about that idea for a moment and thought about how ridiculous it was. "Thanks for the advice, old timer." Cole nodded, turned and started for the door. He could hear the wind continuing to howl outside.

Sheriff Duncan whipped his six gun out of its holster and cocked the hammer back, but Cole did not turn around. "If The Preacher is in this territory, he's my responsibility. I'll get him. Or if you insist on going after him, I'm going with you. What'll it be, Slim?"

Cole cocked his head back but not really looking at Sheriff Duncan and said, "Well, I'm going alone. I have to. It's what I do."

"I knew it," said Duncan. He reholstered his gun. "I'll say a prayer for you anyway. Vaya con dios."

Cole walked out the door and slammed it shut.

Sheriff Duncan stood there looking out the window and said, "Now that's one crazy son of a bitch."

Chapter 13

A Visit from an Old Acquaintance

With his preparations for travel fulfilled, Cole stepped into The Tivoli Saloon across the street from The Byzantium for a much-needed libation. Though he never drank to excess, he enjoyed his whiskey after a task was accomplished. Only a lone bartender occupied the establishment and that was just fine to Cole. He needed space and time to strategize what would be his final journey to secure the future for him and Mattie. He stopped at the bar, ordered his drink and took it to a small table in the back of the barroom. He removed his hat and set it on the table as well.

Outside, a pair of worn hobnail boots pressed down hard on the rotting sidewalk planks. The sound of the boots did not escape Cole. He looked up from his drink and eyed the two swinging doors. His natural reflex kicked in.

Just then, the saloon doors burst open and a booming voice thundered. "I've been lookin' fer you fer ten months! Ever since I got outta that hellhole in Huntsville!" The figure was tall, disheveled and meaner than a rattler. His duster was ripped to shreds, his boot leather torn open in several spots, the rim of his hat covered in sweat stains.

Cole spied the butt of an old model Colt Navy protruding from the holster on his right side. "You talking to me?" asked Cole.

"You remember me?" asked the stranger.

It was at this moment Cole noticed the right sleeve of his duster hung limp and empty.

"You remember me?" shouted the one-armed man.

Cole thought for a minute but he just could not recollect. "I'm sorry but I can't remember every son of a bitch in the Southwest."

The one-armed man grew annoyed and wrinkled his brow as he sneered. "Well, I remember you. Every time I go to sign my name I remember you."

"Why?" asked an equally annoyed Cole.

"As I had to learn how to sign with my right hand!" He held up the empty left hand sleeve.

Cole had learned long ago to remain still in these situations and always look for a weakness. "Hmmm... I see what you mean, but what the hell does this have to do with me?"

The stranger let go of the empty sleeve and fixated on Cole. "Three years ago, you picked me up outside Walker County. It was your bullet that cost me my arm!"

Cole thought hard for a few seconds and then it came to him. "Longhorn Jim McClain! And his Longhorn Boys. Yes, yes. I remember. I guess you should have thought about that before you got into the cattle stealing business. As I recall you and your partners were expert at brand changing."

The one-armed man cracked a sinister grin. "Well, now I'm expert at shootin' with my right hand. Get up, you son of a bitch!"

The barkeep kneeled slowly behind his bar for fear of catching a stray slug.

The one-armed man cleared leather with his Colt Navy.

Cole saw that some of its bluing had come off and then he watched the man pull back the hammer so the gun was fully cocked. The stench of this range bum now permeated the entire saloon. "I'm not responsible for some sawbones' botched job after I turned you in. You know, this doesn't have to happen. You served your time. You could just walk away."

"What are you sayin' to me, BOUNTY WHORE?"

"I'm saying that you could forget all this and just walk away," Cole replied, "grateful." The one-armed man was starting to lose his composure. Cole could always spot when one of these hard cases got rattled. It affected their concentration.

"Grateful for what?"

Cole smiled back at him. "That I don't shoot your other arm off." Cole's hands were under the table, his right nearing slowly to his own iron.

The one-armed man shouted back, "You smug bastard, I spent two years gettin' flogged in that prison…"

"It would be easier if you just walked away." Cole advised. This finally set the man off, his gun hand began to tremble a bit. Cole was trying to get to him.

"Get the fuck up! I'm walkin' you outside of town, then I'll choose which one of yer limbs you'll be losin' in exchange for my arm. Now get up, you son of a bitch!"

Cole leaned calmly back in his chair and stared straight into the man's dead eyes. "You know what my daddy taught me? When you're playing a losing hand, KICK OVER THE TABLE!"

And that's exactly what Cole did. His shot glass flew at the man and the table made a loud crash. Somehow, in only a second, Cole had cleared his weapon, cocked and fired at the one-armed man's heart.

The man never knew what hit him. In his dying seconds his right arm fell to his side and he discharged a round into the floorboards. His body collapsed with all the life drained. Smoke from the black powder filled the room. It smelled a hell of a lot better than the one-armed man.

The barkeep poked his head up from behind the bar. He looked over at Cole. "You was in the right, Mister."

Cole stood up, turned the table right side up and sat back down again. "You better send for that Sheriff Duncan and get this mess cleaned up before this rounder bleeds out all over your parquet floor. I'll have a fresh glass, too."

Just then a voice boomed from outside. "Sheriff Duncan is here!" Duncan threw open the doors and stepped in the saloon. "It's okay, Roscoe. I got the deputies coming over to drag him out of here."

Duncan looked around the room, then looked at Cole. He picked up the thrown shot glass as well as Cole's hat. Walking over to Cole, he brushed the floor dust from the hat's crown. He carefully placed it and the shot glass back on the table. Then he drew up a chair, sat down, produced a half-smoked stogie from his vest pocket and lit it up.

The barkeep, still a bit shaken, approached with a fresh whiskey.

Cole nodded thanks.

Duncan took a deep sigh and drew a big puff off the cigar. "I knew that fella was gonna be trouble when he first rode in."

Cole reacted to Duncan, "Oh, yeah?"

"Yes, sir. He arrived in town about a week after you got patched up at Doc Harrigan's. Asking a lot of questions about you."

"Well, I made $750.00 off his conviction. He might have been kind of bitter about that. They usually are," said Cole.

Sheriff Duncan shook his head. His two deputies arrived and grabbed the body from both ends.

"Take him to Doc Harrigan's, Sheriff?" asked one of the deputies.

"Nah. He's dead meat. Take him to the undertaker's. Use the back door. Chester gets sore when stiffs come in the front. Says it upsets anyone walkin' around the street."

"Yassir, Sheriff." The two deputies carted the one-armed man out like a sack of potatoes.

The Sheriff turned back to Cole. "They're good boys," said Duncan. "Listen, I want to talk to you. First off, as to all this, let me handle it with the judge. He's in Las Cruces anyway. I'll write self-defense on the report. It was. What I'm sayin' is... don't worry about this mess." The Sheriff pointed to where the body had lain. There was a bloodstain about five inches in diameter.

"Oh, I wasn't worried, Sheriff."

Duncan chuckled at that. "Okay. Second, I want to talk to you about this business of yours."

Cole raised an eyebrow and looked at Duncan quizzically. "Didn't we already?"

"I sent a wire to Santa Fe about you. Got a very interesting response. Know what it said? You have a reputation as a very dangerous man. Thank Christ you're on the side of the law. I mean I can see why you have that reputation." Duncan waved again to the bloodstain.

"I spent a lifetime being careful. That's all, Sheriff."

"Right," replied Duncan as there was nothing else to say. "You know, I went out to where you were ambushed."

"Yeah?"

"I found some very strange things out there."

"Such as?"

Duncan reached in his other vest pocket and produced the torn Bible page with the revised scripture written in The Preacher's own hand. He handed it to Cole. "Such as this..."

Cole read the whole page with the strange additions and handed it back to Duncan. "So? I guess he really believes in God."

Duncan stuffed the page back in his vest. "Well, I've been doing some more fact-checking…"

"You people in this town really like to press a point," said an irritated Cole. All he wanted was to be left alone and no one prying into his affairs.

Sheriff Duncan became slightly irritated, too. It was, after all, his job to keep the peace and the citizens safe. "Look, I know you can take care of yourself. I mean, that's obvious. I'm just asking you one more time to let go of this thing. Leave that legend of the strongbox and The Preacher alone. Please! Besides, we're runnin' out of graves on the back side of town."

"I assure you, Sheriff, when it's my time… it ain't gonna be here." Cole pressed his right index finger into the table.

Sheriff Duncan took a different tactic. "What does your woman say?"

A long pause quieted the room and the moment.

"Sheriff, have you ever contemplated atoning for the sins of your life?" asked Cole.

Duncan nodded.

"I may not have much to be proud of but that woman on the second floor of The Byzantium Hotel deserves the best I can provide. I do appreciate your concern, Sheriff. It's downright touching in a way."

"Look, I just…"

Cole cut Duncan off mid-sentence. "I can take care of myself and her. Right now, that's what I intend to do. Adios, Sheriff."

Cole grabbed his hat, took a final belt of what was left of the whiskey, then walked over to the bar counter and plopped a few coins on top. He crossed the room, stopping at the bloodstain on the floor. "And sorry for the mess."

Stepping over the blood, Cole walked outside, the double doors swinging in his wake.

"So long, you crazy bastard," was all Duncan could think of as a response.

Chapter 14

On the Trail

That focused, crazy son of a bitch stubbornly neck-reined Lady onto a narrow trail between two jagged hills. This was not a well-traveled road as the profusion of gypsum weed attested. It had been two days since Cole left Mattie in Sudden and he thought of nothing else but their final moments together – that is, except the quest at hand.

Cole reached into the pocket of his long black frock coat and felt for the document that drove his journey. It was still there, a half-torn map, given to him by a gentle lady of good breeding a few weeks and a few towns ago. This map purported to verify the existence of The Saddle Ridge Horde treasure, long believed to be only a legend. Cole had obtained half of the torn map a week prior to the ambush. Now he rode to secure the remaining portion. The questions remained: was this Preacher character after this legendary fortune and did he already possess the other half of the map?

A half day's ride later, Cole and Lady approached a stream. He let his dark blue roan take a healthy sip from it as he took a swig from his canteen. "Water," he said to Lady. "We must not be far from people now." He pulled his spyglass, expanded it and gazed through it. He spotted a sign on the horizon, which he could not read at this distance. Lady continued to drink from the stream.

What Cole did not notice was high on a ridge behind them was crouched a darkly clad figure who also held a spyglass. Usually Cole was fairly intuitive about being followed, but his mind had been so focused that the thought never occurred to him. The Preacher had been stealthy, he had long ago been a tracker and used those skills to stay just far enough behind Cole's trail so as not to draw attention to his presence. Atop that ridge, The Preacher smiled as he watched the man below. It was a certainty Cole was headed to the next town, a dreary, half-forgotten place named Guilt Ridge, one stop away from his next destination. "He would be in for a surprising disappointment," thought The Preacher. He watched as Cole and his horse moved on.

The Preacher had one more destination to complete the puzzle. He would stay on the ridge and relax a bit. He had time to spare before getting back on the trail. He leaned back and stared at the bright blue sky. His head started to spin and then throb. He heard a ringing in his head. It became so loud he didn't think he would survive the cacophony. It was then that The Preacher had another vision. He saw the sad little boy running through a cotton field. He ran and ran until he came upon the quarters for the plantation field hands. He stood in front of this squalid bunkhouse and listened. He heard sounds, something like moaning. The little boy went inside where he confronted his own father in a compromising sexual situation with a negro woman who served as the field hands' cook.

The big man with the great white beard pulled his trousers up. "I will teach you to spy on adults, you little bastard!" The man grabbed a leather strap from a rein hanging on the wall and began beating the child without pity. "You are an effrontery to God Almighty!" The beating persisted as the negro woman looked on.

The vision continued and suddenly the little boy was crying in his mother's arms. The mother was shouting at the man with the great white beard to no avail. "Your child must learn about sin!" was all he shouted back.

Just as quickly, the woman faded from the vision and appeared in a casket again with mourners filing past. A stern woman stood beside his father and looked down at the little boy.

The vision shifted again, a young man who wore a badge chased a frightened field hand wearing torn rags. The young man's badge read Plantation Police – Runaway Slave Patrol. He cornered the shaking fugitive against a large oak tree. Pulling a bullwhip from his holster and belt, he cracked the whip repeatedly at the frightened black fugitive while ordering him to surrender to his master. The slave catcher placed manacles on the poor man's hands and feet. "This was the way it was before the War of Northern Aggression and it was a good system," thought The Preacher.

The Union victory had made men soft. It was The Preacher's calling to set everything right again. The vision disappeared as quickly as it had come upon him. The horrendous ringing had subsided as well. He took comfort in the idea that much as the renegade faction of Confederates believed The Saddle Ridge Horde would finance a second secession, to get his hands on it would finance The Preacher's dream of setting things right and taming the wicked. He mounted his horse, jammed the Spanish spurs into the beast's belly and took off like lightning.

Meanwhile, Cole approached the outskirts of Guilt Ridge. He passed the sign he spied earlier; the sun-bleached letters of the town name were barely readable. He rode by a graveyard so overgrown by weeds that no markers or headstones were visible. Beyond the graveyard was the last remnants of a structure that had been subjected to fire long ago.

As he entered the main street of town, there were wagon parts, pieces of furniture, an occasional steamer trunk, all just left behind. A deteriorating piano laid on its back in the middle of the street. Each store front was boarded up. The Post Office appeared operational, and so was a small adobe saloon. Two men carried farm implements out of a structure, loading them onto an already full buckboard wagon. "This town should be called 'Abandoned,'" thought Cole. He saw a stage stop at the end of the street, its windows and doors boarded up. He passed a sheriff's office, also locked up tightly, although a decrepit old man sat in front on the sidewalk, spitting on the floorboards.

The wind howled all around the town, spooking Lady.

Chapter 15

The Story of Mattie and Cole

Cole was born somewhere in Illinois. The exact year was unknown, even to him, although it was reckoned to be around November of 1839. His parents were both deceased by 1844. The cause of their deaths were never discussed. After several years, the causes were forgotten. Cole was raised by an aunt and uncle in a rural county. Not until he reached what was thought to be his eleventh birthday did he know that they were not his birth parents. Upon this discovery, some say Cole became despondent and restless.

He attended school held in a church that had very small attendance. Cole's uncle, Zacharias, was an able man, a good man, who instilled the boy with Christian values and morals. When Cole was very young, his uncle/father entered the militia and went off to Mexico during The United States' conflict with that country. While Zacharias was stationed with his regiment in Churubusco, something strange and unforeseen happened. Cole's aunt/mother, Leticia, began entertaining Zacharias' closest friend.

This man had a cooper trade in town for some years and remained free from military service obligation, as his vocation provided an essential service. What began as dinner once a week in the little dining room soon became dinner nightly. Cole watch this strange relationship Leticia had with this man and was puzzled by it. "Shouldn't Pop be coming home soon?" Cole would ask. Zacharias never came home. Every night Cole would be put to bed by Leticia precisely at 7pm. He knew this by the pocket watch Zacharias left behind for him. What happened after 7pm in the small dining parlor or anywhere else in the house for that matter, Cole never knew.

One afternoon, a year later, Cole had walked home from the church/schoolhouse. A rider wearing the uniform of a corporal of the state militia approached the small house. He handed Cole an envelope, saluted the boy and rode off. Cole clutched the envelope closely and ran into the house where Leticia was baking a pie for that night's dinner. She opened the document and read it quietly with no reaction, then stuffed the letter into her apron. That night the man with the cooper trade came to the front door. Leticia greeted him sullenly, though the man did not come in. They stood in the doorway, talking quietly and the man went away. Cole was put to bed at 7 as always.

The next morning, Cole awoke somewhat later than usual. He did not smell the morning coffee, which was ever reliably on the stove, nor whatever would have been frying on the griddle. Cole rubbed his eyes and sauntered to the kitchen. It took him a minute, but soon enough he realized he was alone in the house. He ran into the main bedroom and looked around. Leticia's carpetbag was gone as was a locket she kept on the bureau. It appeared some of her dresses were also gone from the wardrobe closet. He ran back into the kitchen. No signed anything, no note, nothing that might indicate where or why she had left. There was the military envelope delivered by the corporal the previous day. Cole opened it. Proficiently literate since he was about five, he read the letter. It advised that Zacharias would return home from his military service within a fortnight.

Zacharias did eventually return within that time frame. When he walked through the front door, there was young Cole in the small kitchen frying bacon on the griddle and behaving as if everything was under control, which it was. The little house was clean and there was fresh food in the larder. Zacharias asked the boy where the food had come from.

Cole replied, "I walked to town and bought it. I had three shiny silver dollars under my bed I had saved."

Zacharias smiled and yet did not inquire about Leticia's whereabouts. As Cole found out years later, Zacharias rode through town on his way home. It was there that he learned the tale of his pretty young wife and the man with the cooper trade. Neither of them ever discussed it, ever.

Mattie hailed from Lexington, Kentucky where her Baptist father, John, was a successful milliner. It was said he had sold a hat to every woman of societal stature in the Southeast and beyond. Her mother, Dianna, was an outspoken woman who ran an etiquette school for young girls. Unlike Cole, Mattie's birth was well-documented in the month of April in the year 1850. Mattie went to the finest schools and learned French by the time she was ten. She also excelled at mathematics. "She will be a fine woman of society," her mother used to brag to her knitting circle. How wrong Dianna was proven to be.

The War of Northern Aggression visited Lexington in August 1861 when The Lexington Rifles, a pro-Confederacy militia, was formed. Father John immediately enlisted and offered his millinery to the war effort. He made a special trip to Richmond, Virginia for a private meeting with Jefferson Davis in early 1862. John was never seen nor heard from again.

In the ensuing years, Lexington changed hands many times as the Union and John Hunt Morgan's Lexington Rifles took their various turns at occupation. After the surrender, Lexington resembled a declining, dingy widow as did many formerly beautiful Southern cities. During the conflict, Mattie and her mother hung on but when it was all over, there was nothing left.

In the late summer of 1865, Mattie borrowed a pony from a local stable and left Lexington. She had by this time developed a new proficiency. Throughout the years of occupation, she was constantly in contact with soldiers, both Union and Confederate. She favored no side over the other and got on well with all. These soldiers took a liking to young Mattie and they all shared one pastime – card playing. This was the best way to relax between the eruptions of conflict. Mattie learned all the card games from these soldiers as well as some of their tricks and techniques of bluffing.

Dianna adamantly disapproved of playing cards as the devil's handiwork and not appropriate for a lady. As Mattie learned everything about cards, this was to be the breaking point with her mother. Arguments and scoldings were constant in the once-peaceful home that had now fallen into disrepair much like the rest of the once-proud South. So, in that late summer Mattie packed a carpetbag and left on that 'borrowed' pony. Six months later, the stable owner received $75 for the appropriation of the pony, probably $50 more than the pony was worth.

With Mattie's card-playing skills, money seemed to come in easily. Perhaps the presence of a woman in a gambling den distracted the male players. Many gambling halls refused Mattie's entrance. No matter, there were plenty that did not and welcomed the novelty. One such venue was the riverboats. Before the war, these had been fancy floating dens of games of chance. Only the well-heeled, high stakes players could gain access to their plush salons. The war had changed all that; the riverboats were no longer the exclusive floating palaces they once were. Yet, there was still money to be made for those with a keen understanding of a deck of cards. This was where Mattie found herself when a dark stranger entered her life.

Chapter 16

Duncan Has a Chat with Mattie

It was late in the afternoon in Sudden. The waning sun hid behind some clouds and Mattie hid in a corner of the Byzantium Hotel lobby. She sipped tea from a bone china cup, and a shot of whiskey stood next to the cup plate. All she could do was wait. She hated the waiting, always had. While Cole was off on one of his adventures, it took all of her discipline not to worry. She would isolate herself, avoiding people and conversation. Sometimes, she would try reading, but it would never help the longing to see her love return. So she sat, waiting.

Across the street, in the sheriff's office, Sheriff Duncan waited as well. He waited for different reasons: whether this Preacher fellow would come to Sudden, or if Cole returned with his legendary fortune, or some other unexpected result. He just didn't know. Maybe he should visit with that card-playing woman, as they had mutual interests. Duncan rose from his chair, tamped out his cigar, grabbed his hat and sauntered over to The Byzantium.

Once in the lobby, Duncan could not believe his good fortune, Mattie sat there in a corner. He removed his hat and approached her. "Ma'am, may I have a few moments with you?"

"Why?" replied Mattie.

"No particular reason, I just think it might be beneficial to both of us to have a little pow-wow about the situation in general."

Mattie looked at him but did not respond immediately. She waved to an empty chair. "Have a seat, Sheriff."

Duncan sat and rested his hat on the table. He took a moment to gather his thoughts and fired up a fresh stogie. "Your man is stubborn!"

"Hell, I know that, Sheriff."

"I believe in a good way. He loves and cherishes you deeply. I rarely see that anymore, at least around these parts."

"Do you have anyone in your life, Sheriff?" Mattie asked.

Duncan leaned back and smiled. "I did, once upon a time. I was young, full of the zest of life, looking forward to all it had to offer. I suppose as the years went on, I became distracted, focused on everything else except her. She sensed it and that was how I lost her. My life has been a solitary one ever since. I never found another woman. Hell, I didn't even try to look."

"That's a shame, Sheriff."

"No, not really. It has been a good life. I have no regrets," Duncan said. "Some time ago, I realized that I was destined to be alone in this mortal existence."

"Are you not lonely?"

"I'm comfortable!" said Duncan jovially.

"How did you come to lose her, Sheriff?" Mattie inquired.

Duncan was unused to personal conversation and inquiries, yet he felt a bond with this woman and her man, even if he did not know why. "I met her during my military service. In '62 I was serving with the Dakota Campaign with General Sibley. When we arrived at Fort Snelling, there was a captain with a beautiful daughter named Clara. She was the loveliest girl I had ever laid eyes on. Sixteen years old. We courted briefly but then I shipped out. I returned to the fort six weeks later. She had just turned seventeen and we married. I spent the rest of the war up there in Minnesota moving The Dakota Tribe around, never saw any action in the national conflict. While I resided in the fort, Clara lived in a nearby rooming house with the other wives. We saw each other every Saturday for the regiment dances and every Sunday for church. It was heaven. Then, I mustered out in '64, my service obligation fulfilled."

Mattie had by this time finished her tea and took a healthy sip of the whiskey.

Duncan continued, "Here I was with a now 18-year-old bride, $35.00 in my poke and not a glimmer of an idea where we were going. Heard stories about a shortage of men for law dogs due to the war. I thought, hell, that sounds like something steady. We drifted down Kansas way, doing all kinds of odd jobs en route. When we hit Abilene, I managed to get sworn in as a deputy sheriff almost immediately. The cattle markets were really coming into their own and the sheriff needed men as the town was growing. Clara and I lived in a small rooming house. I think we were the happiest then. Clara always had a fresh cactus rose on the little dining table every day when I'd come home. Then... I went and did it."

"What?" asked Mattie.

"The old sheriff, a fella named Pemberton, announced he was retiring, leaving the position of sheriff vacant. So... I announced myself as a candidate!" said Duncan. "Ran against some jasper named Middleton who had a terrible penchant for alcoholic spirits. Maybe that was why I beat him in the election. So there I was, the new sheriff of Abilene. I did not know what was in store for me! As the cattle market wildly expanded, so did the number of ne'er-do-wells who visited town. Soon, almost overnight, the saloons increased as well as the gambling halls and the joy houses. Soon Abilene was swarming with wild cowhands, crooked peddlers, unscrupulous trail bosses, and a collection of saddle tramps and miscreants the likes of which you could never imagine. Shootings were a daily occurrence, along with robberies and cattle theft. I had to hire on five new deputies just to handle the load!"

Sheriff Duncan paused. He collected his thoughts and continued, "After two years of this, Clara started to worry. She'd often go without sleep for days, many times when I hit the trail after some fugitive desperado. Then, one night in the alley behind The Lost Lug Saloon, I shot four hard cases who were gunnin' for me as I had their rustler leader locked in my jail. That was it, I told Clara the next day. I handed my badge to the mayor, a sickly fella with a tapeworm. 'We'll double your pay, Duncan!' he said. I told him no amount of money was worth that kinda trouble. So, I bought an old buggy and hitched up my own horse and we skedaddled out of Abilene with what little possessions we had. Wound up in a place called Elizabethtown, here in the territory."

"I know it," said Mattie. "It smells and the gambling hall perpetually sinks beneath the ground."

"Yes, ma'am. That is the place. They had back-to-back copper and gold strikes. I went to work for one of the big mining concessions there as... what would I call it? An enforcer? It was then I started learning that miners were no better than cattlemen regarding morality. In fact, the gold fever made 'em worse! Just about this time, I had quite a dust-up with some derelict tin-panners who were disputing a stake with another claim-holder. One thing led to another and fisticuffs broke out. I showed up to the scene and then they all cleared leather and started shootin' at me. I plugged all six of 'em. The territorial judge said it was a clear case of self-defense. That night I went back to our little rooming house, which was nothing more than a wood frame with canvas draped over it and canvas interior walls. Clara informed me her cousin was visiting the army barracks in the next county. She planned to leave the next morning and spend a week with him. I wondered how she knew this as I didn't recall any correspondence between the two of them. So, the next morning, she took the same little buggy and a mule we had somehow acquired and left. As I waved her off, I had an uneasy feeling."

Mattie drained the last remnants of the whiskey. "What happened then?"

"She never came back. I waited, but no word ever came," Duncan replied. "I rode to that army barracks and asked the commandant about it all. The cousin bivouacking there, my wife's arrival, everything. He said he had no records of Clara's cousin and further stated Clara had never been seen by him nor any of his men. I went back to Elizabethtown, quit my job and set out looking for Clara. I searched for six months. Never found her, no trace, no clue. I stopped in some place called Splendour because they had a postal office. After writing a letter to her father back in Minnesota, I rented a room behind a hardware store and waited. I know I included a return address to the local saloon there. I heard nothing. Weeks went by. I was runnin' low on coin so I took a job as a payroll escort for the local express office. More weeks went by. On one of my payroll runs, one of the drivers told me they'd been looking for a new sheriff in Sudden about twenty miles down the road. I quit my job, left Splendour and rode to Sudden. When I arrived, I went to the mayor's house. Sudden lost its sheriff six months previous and some fairly shady characters had drifted into town and started pushin' people around. The mayor swore me in almost immediately, no election, no town council vote. I've been here ever since."

Mattie looked directly at Duncan. "Did you ever find Clara?"

"Nope. Wrote a new forwarding address to her father but still never had a response."

"How did you live with it, Sheriff?"

"I lived with it. I guess if it was meant to be, I would have found her," Duncan said. "In a way, I can't blame her. Other than our first days together, I never provided her with what she really wanted. I just kept coming up short. I reckon the gunplay got to her as well."

Mattie reflected on this. Of course the gunplay got to Clara; it got under Mattie's skin, too. She sensed a parallel life with Duncan. It was all the uncertainty and the danger. "You don't have something else you want to peddle, sheriff?"

"What else would I have to say? I would have wished I could stop your man from taking on this hunt. I didn't sway him and he's gone. I hope God is watching out for him."

Mattie fought back a tear. She tipped the whiskey glass to her lips but the amber elixir was no more. "Sheriff, you may be right. Sometimes, just talking does a wealth of good. I don't mind confessing that I always worry just a bit when Cole is off on one of his fortune hunts but this one scares me, and I don't scare easy!"

"Ma'am, all we can do is pray. Pray and wait. That's what I've been doing all these years."

"And did it do you any good, Sheriff?"

Duncan tamped out his cigar. He paused for a moment and leaned back in his chair. "Whether it produces any good result is now irrelevant. I just do it as a matter of habit. Sometimes, it's just the action and not the result that counts."

"Sheriff, life is a tragic, lonely business."

"I fear you may have a point there, ma'am."

"Our joy is short-lived but our pain endures endlessly," said Mattie in a low voice. "But we keep saying the prayer anyway."

Chapter 17

The Continuing Story of Mattie and Cole

Cole had never been on a riverboat, he had no reason. He was always an overland traveler. Occasionally, he traveled by rail but for the most part he preferred the freedom of the outdoors sitting tall in his Hope saddle on his blue roan named Lady. Cole and Lady had travelled far and wide together. This was the first time, however, either of them had been in Tennessee. Cole rarely left the Southwest. But an interesting handbill caught his eye in a marshal's office in Fort Smith, Arkansas. Cole had just delivered a fugitive to him.

"Tell me about this leg bailer, Marshal," Cole asked as he pointed to a handbill on the wall.

"A real hard case, son. Chance McCulloch," replied the Marshal.

"Reason he's got the moniker 'Chance?'" asked Cole.

"Fancies himself a professional gambler. Has a pretty good reputation as one. He's wanted for over twenty-five charges from here to California."

"Violent?" asked Cole.

"When necessary. Known more as a confidence artist, although a number of his plays resulted in homicide," warned the Marshal sternly. "He's personally sent two sheriffs and three Pinkertons to the bone yard."

Cole rubbed his beard and then shifted his hat while studying the handbill.

"He's worth $2000.00 if you can corner him. He's fairly squirrelly, though."

"They all are," said Cole before tearing the handbill off the wall.

So, this was the reason Cole and Lady were riding into the city of Memphis. Chance McCulloch was last seen headed into Tennessee and was likely to ply his gambling tricks on a riverboat. Cole confirmed this with the Marshal in Fort Smith before he set out.

Once in Memphis, Cole boarded Lady and stowed his tack and personal effects. He registered in a room in a small hotel, took a much needed bath, and threw together an appropriate wardrobe for boarding a riverboat. He never wore much finery; mostly his preferred clothing was range wear complemented by a long town coat or maybe a duster. He settled on a black frock coat, dark gray pullover shirt, black trousers and a pair of black town boots. He looked in the mirror and decided not to shave. Overall, he looked the very definition of darkness. He packed a compact hideaway Smith pistol rather than his preferred .44 with the snake inlay grip. Everything else he put in stow over at the stable with Lady.

That night, The Empress steamed her way to the Memphis dock. Several passengers disembarked. Ticket in hand, the small gun tucked in his waistband, Cole boarded the ship. An hour later, The Empress steamed away and Cole made his way to the gambling salon. There were five tables in the salon, all of them full with card sharpies. One table stood out as a beautiful woman with long straw-colored hair dealt stud poker. "This is unusual," thought Cole. "What was a woman doing in the salon?"

He scanned each table for Chance McCulloch, remembering his physical description: "nose bent hideously to the right, pock-marked face." No one seemed to fit that description at first, but then he spotted him – at the table with the woman dealer! He watched as she dealt the cards with some flourish, speaking all the while, a known card player trick of distraction.

Cole approached the table. "Excuse me, sir, you are wanted in the purser's office," he said behind McCulloch's back.

Chance McCulloch snapped back, "I don't give a two-penny damn. Can't you see I'm busy, jasper?"

Cole place a firm hand on McCulloch's shoulder. "Now would be a good time to excuse yourself. The house will see after your funds."

"Gentlemen, may I suggest a one hour break for refreshment or sustenance?" said the woman with the straw-colored hair.

"Good for me," said McCulloch.

"I agree," uttered the other two players.

Cole escorted McCulloch out of the gambling salon into an adjacent drawing room where he flipped him around. Drawing a handbill from his coat, he handed it to McCulloch. As he unfurled it, McCulloch's eyes widened, then squinted when he looked directly back at Cole.

"Hell, you gotta be joking, buster!"

"No... I am very serious," replied Cole.

"You expect to haul me all the way back to Fort Smith? You're on a boat, goin' the opposite way! Pea-brained son of a bitch!"

Cole smiled, "No, actually I plan on turning you in to the Pinkerton office in Memphis or the next river stop."

"You daft bastard, you'll never get me off this boat!"

"We'll see about that."

Just then Chance McCulloch jerked his right arm forward and a knife slipped easily into the palm of his hand. He lunged at Cole, who was about to draw his pocket Smith. The knife connected with Cole's wrist and drew blood.

"Stop! The both of you!" The card-playing woman stood before them, a two shot derringer in her right hand.

"You two in cahoots?" yelled McCulloch.

"Nope. Never seen this gentleman before!" she said.

McCulloch lunged at both of them, knife favoring Cole and that was the moment the woman with the straw-colored hair shot him in the foot. McCulloch collapsed in pain.

"We better fetch the boat's doctor," she said.

"Yeah... or this son of a bitch will bleed all over this fine Persian rug. What's your name?" asked Cole.

"Mattie," said the woman.

"I'd be Cole. I'm here to apprehend this man in the name of the law. He has quite a few charges hung around his neck and he's also wanted by the Pinkertons. Known hard case and a slippery bastard."

"Good thing I was here then!" Mattie declared. "Also be a good idea to get the sawbones to wrap that hand."

Chapter 18

Duncan and the Deacons

Sheriff Duncan once read in a Pinkerton manual: "the investigation never rests." With this thought in mind, what could be the harm in riding out to the site where Cole had been ambushed one more time? Perhaps he missed some clue or piece of evidence as to the whereabouts of this strange Preacher character. After all, this ambush and shooting happened within his jurisdiction; he, alone, should be responsible for dispensing justice. So, he saddled up Buck and rode out to the ambush site.

As Duncan rode the same trail up the hill outside of town, the wind stirred up with that same plaintive wail. Buck started to rear up.

"Easy there, big fella. It ain't nothin' but the wind."

Other sounds mixed with the wind – trees swaying, crows cawing, wild sounds that belonged in a nightmare. Duncan came upon what appeared to be a campsite gone cold, the remnants of a fire, a few blankets and some tin cups and plates. Now who the hell would stop here, he thought. He gave Buck a gentle kick and moved on.

A few hundred feet down the trail he hit the crest of the hill, instantly spotting the makeshift pulpit. Riding towards it, he discovered a sheaf of papers bundled together. Stopping Buck, he dismounted and walked over to the discovery. What he saw did not surprise him. The papers contained twisted versions of scripture much like the previously discovered document.

Grabbing Buck's left rein, Duncan read through the documents as he walked to the makeshift pulpit. The words conjured up imagery that was horrifying: great beasts, descriptions of Hell, methods of execution, graphic descriptions of sins – it was all sickening.

As he walked on with Buck at his side, a voice boomed out of nowhere, cutting through the whining wind. "Stand fast!"

Duncan stopped in his tracks. He checked his surroundings yet found no one.

The voice boomed again, "What do you want?"

"I am Sheriff Duncan from Sudden. It's just over the hill." Duncan gestured behind him even though he saw no one. The wind died down and silence ensued for what seemed like an eternity. Then he heard footsteps trampling over brush. He tried to count the steps to ascertain how many men it might be.

"Here we be!"

Duncan whirled to his right where the voice seemed to be. What he saw was a curious sight. Two men wearing odd garments stood before him. The first man, the taller of the two, wore all black and a frayed top hat with a bone stuck in the hat band. His ankle-length black coat, also frayed, displayed embroidered symbols all over it such as crucifixes, demons, and skulls. The second man wore stovepipe boots, filthy, gray trousers and a faded frock coat that had once been white. Both men were armed.

"So you be a local sheriff?" The first man put his hands on his hips and tilted his head sideways. The tension grew thick.

"I am. Who are you boys?"

"Servants of God. That is, God as we understand him."

"I didn't know that kind of thing was up for interpretation," said Duncan.

The first man showed outrage. He stared at Duncan as if trying to bore through him with his eyes. "I am Brother Greed and this is Brother Malice." He gestured to the man in the faded frock coat who began to scream gibberish. Throwing his arms upward, the second man stomped his feet like some strange dance and turned around in a full circle, an upside down red cross was painted on the backside of his frock coat. Walking up to Duncan, he screamed something incoherent at him. He smelled like a goat. Then he backed off.

"I'm sorry, I don't understand your friend here," Duncan said.

"That's fine, Mister. I do, that's all that matters."

"What are you boys doing up here?"

"Oh, this? It is one of our places of worship" said Brother Greed.

"Just you two up on this hill?" Sheriff Duncan's right hand still held the rein, while his left held the sheaf of papers. Clearly, the drop was on him. He had to be ready, have a plan, in case these jaspers drew on him.

"As servants to His Holiness, The Preacher, we are never alone!" Brother Greed raised his hands to the firmament. Brother Malice cackled and mumbled.

"So that's your game... The Preacher. Well, boys, I'm on a mission to find out where your boss might be."

"I see you have some of our Holy Scriptures."

Duncan held up the papers, "Oh, these things? Couldn't make heads or tails out of this tripe."

The two men's brows wrinkled, Duncan struck a nerve. "Sir, you are obviously not enlightened. These are the sacred writings of our Holy One."

"I'll stick with the traditional source. Call me old school," responded Duncan.

Brother Greed stepped forward. He began to walk in a circle around Duncan, his hand near his pistol. "That is the fly in the buttermilk, people not understanding the true word. We get that a lot. For years we have been on this holy journey with The Preacher and it still shocks me how little the word and the light are accepted. These poor lost souls fritter away their existence never knowing, never curious, wholly unaccepting. Shocking, absolutely shocking. To combat this, we have very strict methods of enforcing the truth and the light. Consequences for unacceptance can be harsh... to say the least. Punishment can be very ugly as well as painful. Does that not make you desirous, wicked one, to accept the truth and the light?"

Duncan sized him up as the greater threat of the two. He dropped the rein and the papers simultaneously, but gently. Then like a flash, Brother Greed drew a knife from his belt and threw it. The blade pierced the sheaf of papers with a ping.

"Now that is what I mean. That might have hurt just a few inches closer to you." Brother Greed continued circling.

"Maybe it's your method that discourages folks from accepting your word. Bit of a hard sell if you ask me," Duncan said.

Brother Greed tilted his head in that weird fashion again. Duncan had gotten to him. "Well, I ain't asking, law dog. You know, I spent several years in a place down South where I was not allowed to speak or even think. They fed us gruel and stale mutton. There was a man in this place who called himself a doctor but he never healed anybody. Then one day, a quiet man arrived who was to change the course of every man's life in that place. He turned out to be a great man! For years I was called insane, this man enlightened me that I was gifted. He saved the two of us! Since our deliverance from that terrible place we have been saving souls."

"You must be referring to that Preacher fellow. What about those who do not want to be saved?"

"Well, they forfeit their right to mortal existence..." said Brother Greed with a grin.

"What choice are you giving me?"

"I'm not sure I will give you a choice. No, sir, I don't much care for your attitude. Nor your disrespect. Now then, what shall be done with you? What indeed?" Greed's hand edged closer to his sidearm. Brother Malice went back into his dance and spewing his gibberish.

This was Duncan's chance. Time to seize the advantage. Like a flash of lightning, he drew his Colt, wheeled around and pumped two cartridges into Greed. Then he swung back, extended his gun hand and fired at Malice who had already drawn, hitting his left shoulder. The man buckled, but pulled himself up and fired a badly placed shot in Duncan's general direction. The bullet ricocheted off a nearby rock.

Duncan fired again hitting the babbling wretch, but he knew not where. "Had enough, you donkey-dancing bastard?" Duncan held his Colt firmly.

Brother Malice started to weep and, just like that, he took off in a weak run, arms flailing.

"Go ahead, run. You're half-dead, anyway."

Duncan holstered his Colt and walked over to the body of Greed to make sure he was dead, and to check for clues. None would be found except a hand-drawn picture of a strange looking cathedral. He had no shovel as he did not anticipate a burial. Perhaps he could cover the body with rocks. Best to leave him, Duncan thought. The buzzards would do the work for him. They have to eat just like everybody else.

Chapter 19

The Middle of Nowhere

The sun beat down over an endless horizon of sand dunes. An occasional dust devil kicked up every now and then. Lady carried Cole through this surreal landscape with her head high. Hours faded by. The scenery changed, scrub trees and other shrubs now dotted the landscape, which meant water could not be far and where there was water there were people.

Riding over a small ridge, there appeared a railroad track, narrow gauge, old and neglected, definitely long out of commission. The rusty tracks led to the horizon where there appeared a hazy profile of what looked like a cluster of shacks or buildings.

Cole had found it! The next destination in his journey for that long-dreamed better life for him and Mattie.

The town of Bliss had been founded after the discovery of what was believed to be a large potash deposit in the area. A series of ramshackle structures went up and the town of Bliss was born. A perceived silver strike brought a narrow gauge rail line from the main line some 20 miles away. It was a strange little boomtown with the usual complement of boarding houses, bordellos, and gambling dens. Incredibly there was even a tiny opera house built. Spectators, driven by avarice, sunk many dollars into the area, hoping, praying that Bliss could be the new Santa Fe. That never happened. By 1870, the potash ore deposits fizzled out and the little silver to be extracted from the earth proved meaningless. The railroad closed the spur line and Bliss started choking a rapid death. The people left in droves, mostly leaving their stores, belongings and furnished shacks behind. In a few years, Bliss went from a population of 2000 to 50.

One of the last holdouts was Bonnie Blue Jacoby. She owned the general mercantile store and she stayed because she was trapped. The years had not been kind to her. Her body and face wore the scars of abuse, mostly administered by her former husband, Colonel Everett Jacoby of the late Confederacy. She was the next piece in the puzzle of Cole's journey.

Cole drew his spyglass from its pommel case. Pulling the lens to his right eye, he viewed the town in the distance. Slapping the scope to its collapsed position, he announced proudly to Lady, "Well, we found it, girl!" They rode into the town of Bliss, the last known residence of Bonnie Blue Jacoby. Once in the main and seemingly only street in the town, the structures looked much bigger than on the horizon and gave the eerie impression of tilting inward over the only street like tinder monsters worn by neglect and time.

"I've been in some ugly places, Lady, but this one takes the cake." Cole remembered seeing illustrations of a dead, decomposed whale and that's what this place looked like. A few faces peered out of the various windows, a swayback horse threw its tail swatting flies, a blind man sat under an eave on which a sign read "Haberdashers" with the last "s" hanging precariously upside down. Cole rode to the man and asked, "Town of Bliss?"

"Ain't the sign outside town still? Hell, I haven't seen nothin' in two years. Took blind from some bad hooch," replied the old man. He slapped his cane twice for no particular reason.

"Well, you ain't missing much, Gramps," said Cole. "General store still here?"

"Yassir, end of the street, Jacoby's Mercantile."

"Thank you, sir." If the other half of the map existed, it was in that general store.

The old man spat and said nothing.

Cole rode to the end of the street, passing one empty storefront after another, and there it was. A few doors down, he spotted what he came for – "Jacoby's Mercantile." He rode Lady up to the hitching post and jumped off. Using a getaway hitch, he secured Lady to the rail. Cole stepped up a wooden plank platform and dusted the roadside off himself. "You stay here, Lady."

A strange, wiry man wearing long johns, trousers supported by suspenders and worn miner boots came at him. The man clutched a toy doll and muttered some kind of gibberish. Cole just stared at him for a moment and walked on.

The weird man ran away but turned and shouted, "Death is everywhere!"

Cole ignored the man and opened the door to the general store. A small bell tinkled as the door opened. The store was bigger inside than it looked on the outside, maybe as a result of so little merchandise in stock. A woman, worn beyond her years, folded fabric behind a counter. She turned, revealing a black cloth eyepatch over her right eye.

"What can I do for you, handsome?" The woman spat tobacco juice into a spittoon and it rang out.

Cole surveyed the whole store and its contents. "I'd be looking for something special."

"Well, pretty slim pickings here. Haven't needed to order goods from my drummer in a coon's age. Been that way since they took the rail line and the stage stop away."

"Well, I'm not looking for any regular stock merchandise."

"Name's Bonnie Jacoby. So what the hell is it you're lookin' for, Slim?"

"Hear tell that you can show me the other half of this." Cole reached into his long coat and pulled out a document made of parchment paper. It was one half of a detailed, hand-drawn map ripped, apparently, right down the center.

Bonnie's eyes widened in astonishment as she looked at the parchment. "God's holy trousers... where in hell did you get that?"

"Name is Cole. I'm looking for the other half."

"Did you know my late husband?"

Cole still held the map tightly. "Can't say I did."

Bonnie spat the last of the tobacco juice out into the spittoon. "That's a plus in your favor. Had you known that double-dealing polecat, I would throw your sorry ass outta here. You ain't lyin'... are ya?"

"No, ma'am," Cole shot back.

Bonnie studied Cole up and down trying to make some kind of character judgment. "You got an honest face, more important, an honest look in your eyes." She paused for a few moments, then let out her revelation, "You must've hornswoggled that from Sadie, am I right?"

"No ma'am, I paid her fair and square. Would you care to see the bill of sale?" Cole reached back into his coat.

"No... I believe you, but Sadie is too wise to give up anything for free. Must've done her a real good turn." Bonnie went back to sizing up Cole. "Did you fuck her?"

Cole was taken aback by this query. "Nothing of the sort! I just helped her out of a tight spot, I guess."

"What are you? Some kind of shootist? She's the type of old gal who'd need one of them... all her enemies!"

Cole put the map back in his coat for safety. He thought carefully. "When someone hires me, I like to keep it discreet."

"Well, then, 'Mr. Discreet,' I suppose you know that Sadie and I were married to the same man?"

"Yep."

"AT THE SAME DAMN TIME!"

"They call it bigamy, " Cole said quietly.

"Well, I call it bullshit! We were both wed to Colonel Jacoby of the late Confederacy. You know about his role in The Knights of the Golden Circle?"

"I do."

Bonnie came around to the front of the counter, grabbed the stub of a cigar, lit it and sat in a chair. "Why don't you tell me..."

Cole turned directly to Bonnie. "The Knights of the Golden Circle was a pre-war secessionist league. Mired in secrecy, steeped in codes and shadowy doings. Their mission was to extend slavery through Mexico and the Caribbean. After Appomattox, they made off with quite a haul from the Confederate treasury in Richmond. This map shows the resting place of the Saddle Ridge Horde. Moved around a dozen or more times in the hopes of financing a second secession."

Bonnie nodded her head in approval. "What makes you think I don't want to get my hands on it?"

Cole leaned into her. "Fear... and your abject hatred for the late Colonel Jacoby."

"True. My late husband... our late husband... Sadie'n me... was a bastard. I had two eyes like everybody else when I started that marriage. He beat me something fierce. Was the only way he could get it... well, you understand...."

Cole looked at the pain in her one eye. Suffering was something he knew so much about but this was about as cruel as he had yet witnessed. "You don't have to talk about it. Sadie told me that the two of you were out to discredit his wartime record and legacy, and in the process destroy the last vestiges of that secret society."

Tears began to well up in Bonnie's left eye but she caught herself and took a big, spirited puff from the cigar stub. Still, her voice cracked from the pain. "True. I hated every last thing that man stood for. Why the hell should I help you?"

"I can't think of a reason in the world."

"You know what I say, Mister? That map ain't worth horse piss. Fact is, I don't reckon there ever was any gold coins in that Saddle Ridge Horde. I believe it was all doodle-squat to keep them boys from the South hangin' onto a dream. A dream that ain't never gonna come true." She paused, taking another puff from the stogie. "You got yourself a woman?"

"The finest in all 37 states!"

"Then, what the hell you want with this bad business?"

"You are not the first to ask that. I reckon that ill-gotten money can go to a worthy cause for a change. A new life for Mattie and me."

"That's an honest answer. So, now, I am gonna be honest with you. You're too late. I ain't got it."

"What do you mean?"

"A fella was here a few weeks ago. Real mean son of a bitch. I sold it to him. He paid me in Mexican gold coins. It's enough for me to get the hell out of here. Had you come this way at this time tomorrow, I would have been long gone." Bonnie rose up and walked behind the counter. She stared out the window. "On my way north to Chicago where I'll be wearing a velvet dress and living like a lady again."

Cole thought for a moment and asked, "Was this man a... preacher?"

Bonnie spun around.

"Sure as hell was, but real strange. Never heard no preacher talk like him before. I think he knew Colonel Jacoby during the war. Seems loony now."

Cole sighed, "Well, I guess there is nothing for me, then. I thank you, Ma'am, for your time." Cole tipped his hat and turned towards the door.

"Just a minute, shootist! Come back here."

Cole turned and looked at Bonnie.

"Don't you think I remember everything about that goddamn map? Come back here and I'll tell you the secrets of The Knights of the Golden Circle."

<hr>

When Cole mounted Lady, he had both halves of the map, half on parchment and half burned into his memory. Poor Bonnie must have spent hours and years staring at that half with her hatred growing. Cole offered to pay her or do her a service but Bonnie wouldn't have any of it. She was right, the Colonel was a real bastard. Two wives and the map split between them. As he rode away, he thought of their final exchange.

"Hey, Mister, you better say a prayer."

"Why, ma'am?"

"Because it ain't there. Don't exist."

"If that's true, then I just move on."

"Say a prayer anyway, for yourself, cowboy."

As they rode out of range of the strange town of Bliss, Cole hoped Bonnie would be living like a lady again and soon. He decided he'd pray for that.

Chapter 20

A Genteel Lady of Society

Sadie Jacoby's home sat outside the town center of Santa Fe. Elegant and palatial, the Victorian structure symbolized class and wealth. Many a member of "polite society" passed through its large, double front doors. Sadie welcomed all manner of politicos, business barons, even European royalty. She was considered the "hostess" of Santa Fe.

On this particular afternoon she was a hostess to horror. Earlier that morning, The Preacher had sent a boy from his hotel to give word to Mrs. Jacoby that he would pay her a visit that afternoon. She confirmed that she would receive him and sent the boy back to the hotel with the message. Sadie had her housemaid prepare a tea service with cakes in the parlor.

At the prescribed time, a violent knock at the big double doors echoed through the foyer. Sadie walked to the doors and opened one to reveal The Preacher in all his dark finery. He tipped his wide brimmed black hat and bowed.

"Hello," said Sadie. "The boy from the hotel said you'd be over and here you are. Come in, please." She gestured towards the parlor and The Preacher walked in. All was silent until they were seated across from one another with the tea service between them. Sadie poured two cups as the silence was broken.

"The Lord and I give thanks that you would see me on this matter, Mrs. Jacoby."

"Please, please, dispense with the formality, Parson. Call me Sadie. I am a churchgoer myself. I take great pride in it. What denomination do you represent?"

The Preacher paused a moment, carefully crafting his answer. "I have my own flock, a relatively new order in the Southwest."

"Your letter said you knew my late husband."

"Yes, I served in Colonel Jacoby's regiment. That is until I was captured outside of Vicksburg. I spent the balance of the conflict in a Union prisoner of war camp. Not a pretty story... for such a pretty lady." His charm was in full flourish and working on Sadie.

"So what is it I may help you with?"

"I am writing my memoirs of the late war between the states," lied The Preacher.

"Seems most of the generals have beaten you to that! All except our own territorial governor General Wallace, whom I hear tell is working on a grand biblical epic tome called *Ben-Hur*."

"More specifically, I am interested in a secret organization in which your husband was an officer and founding member."

Sadie responded with some disdain, "Oh, that. Well that is a painful memory for me. I never like to speak of..."

"Please, Mrs. Jacoby!" Interrupted The Preacher. "All due respect to your emotions, I am willing to pay handsomely for access to the Colonel's papers."

"Parson, please. This is a raw subject with me." Sadie was becoming furious, this was not what she expected.

"Do not disappoint me. I have traveled some distance at considerable cost to gain this audience with you," explained The Preacher.

"You make this sound urgent, Parson."

"It may be."

Sadie relented and sighed, "Since you are most insistent, I shall fetch his document box."

The Preacher stood as she rose and walked into an adjacent room. During her absence, he perused a local news periodical pretending to read it while actually taking in the surroundings and all the precious objects around the room. He noted the former Colonel's cavalry sword perched on the mantle.

Sadie reentered the parlor carrying a tin box.

The Preacher stood again and the two sat down.

Sadie produced a small key and inserted it in a lock, then flipped the lid open. She ran her fingers through the stack of papers, tintypes and military communiques. "This contains my late husband's documents and correspondence pertaining to the war... and that damned society he chartered."

Sadie paused and held up a photograph of a young enlisted man. On the back of the photograph was scrawled the word "villain." She looked at The Preacher and then again at the photograph with a wary eye.

"May I see the contents?" The Preacher extended his right arm across the table.

Sadie continued to hold the picture while looking at him. "You said you were in a prisoner of war camp up north?"

"I did."

Sadie stared again at the picture. "Strange, no, it could not be."

"Please Mrs. Jacoby. Time is of the essence!"

"Is this about that Saddle Ridge of coins? That damned map?" Sadie had her dander up.

"Madam, I am sure I do not know of what you speak," The Preacher answered.

"IT IS YOU! You were a slave catcher before the war. My husband told me about you and your unspeakable acts. You lynched seven slaves and a plantation foreman in Mississippi for collaborating with a Union patrol. Your depravity sickened even the most hardened rebel. You were hauled off and sent to a sanitarium in Louisiana. My God... and I allowed you into my home. Well, Mr. Preacher, my husband was a very dangerous man who led a duplicitous life. I learned a thing or two about survival from him."

The Preacher now unleashed his rage. "YOUR HUSBAND OFFENDED THE LORD WITH HIS BIGAMY! Now I have come here on a specific holy purpose. I will advise you to to acquiesce to my inquiry. IMMEDIATELY!"

Sadie sank back into the cushions of the divan. She was frightened. "I know my life has been a sinful lie," she said. "But there is nothing that can be done, nothing to your inquiry can be answered."

"What the hell do you mean?"

"There was a man, a good man, who helped me settle the accounts with the other evil men of my late husband's past. That chapter of my life is over and I have devoted the balance of my mortality to righteousness and pure deeds."

"Who is this man and what does he have to do with the other half of THIS?" The Preacher produced and held up the half of the map he purchased from Bonnie, thrusting it into Sadie's face.

"I... I... gave this man the other half of that map..."

"That is unfortunate for you, dear lady. Do you recall any of its directions or markings?"

"I do not."

"That is even more unfortunate."

"You are as crazy as a peach orchard boar. Get out of my house!" Sadie demanded.

"Not until I have had a thorough search of the premises and I have exhausted your memory." The Preacher drew a long blade Bowie knife. He rose up and began tearing up the parlor. When that was done, he moved to the next room.

A housemaid ran into the parlor to see what all the commotion was about.

The sound of glass breaking, plus Sadie and her housemaid screaming, were the sounds of the rest of that afternoon.

⸺⳥⳥⳥⳥⸺

A week later, a messenger from a local attorney's office came by to deliver some legal documents to the Jacoby residence. He noticed the front double doors wide open, and went inside to look for Sadie. What he found was the whole house in shambles, with the floors being a litter of glass, china, torn books, and other debris. The housemaid and Sadie were nowhere to be found, at least not immediately. A little later, the housemaid was discovered strung upside down hanging from a eucalyptus tree. And Sadie was found at the bottom of the well.

The Preacher was long gone.

Chapter 21

The Big Discovery

Cole's head relaxed on his saddle, which was now on the ground. Lady drank from a small creek a few feet away. He held a tintype of Mattie in his left hand, his right hand near the cross draw holster out of habit. As he looked at the tintype, he imagined the location of The Saddle Ridge Horde should be dead ahead over that ridge.

He rode up and over it and came smack in front of an old mine entrance. Stuffing the compass into his saddlebag, he dismounted and let Lady's reins drop to the ground. She would be just fine out here and Cole was careful that no one had followed him. He produced a small lantern from the saddlebag and lit it with a match, then proceeded into the mine entrance.

Once inside, all Cole's wits were working. It would not do to have come this far and suffer a cave-in or animal attack. He moved just a few feet inside past cobwebs and other debris, such as old shovels and picks. Then, just past a rusted mine cart, there it was, a metal grate with a rusted lock on it. The grate had a Greek symbol on it probably representing The Knights of the Golden Circle. Cole had no idea of its translation, but he sensed this must be the resting place. He moved the lantern up to the the metal bars and he could see a cavity in the mine wall and a square object inside.

Most mines emit toxic and combustible gases so Cole made sure this one was devoid of any such problem. If he fired his gun in proximity to these gases, the whole thing could blow sky high, but according to the legend on the map, this mine had been inactive for years. He reckoned he was in the clear and blew the lock apart with one shot from his .44. He pulled the grate off and it fell to the ground with a clang.

Next he put his leather gloves on. Reaching into this thing, it would not do to run into a scorpion or tarantula. He grabbed the worn leather

handle and slid the strongbox slowly out. Using every bit of strength, he yanked it out and it fell to the ground on top of the grate.

Cole started dragging it outside. "Jesus, goddamn thing weighs as much as my horse!"

Once outside, he assessed the situation. There was a hasp with another lock hanging from the metal loop. These rebel boys sure were not much for security! Removing his gloves, he stuffed them into his belt. Drawing his .44 again, he raised his left hand to his face to deflect any flying debris or powder blowback. The gun fired and echoed throughout the gully. Lady raised her head to see what the commotion was about. The lock blown to hell, Cole kicked the lid to the strongbox and it flew open with a metallic ring. Lady looked up again.

A gauze-like fabric lay on the top of the contents. Cole kneeled and tore the gauze away. It was what was probably left of a deteriorated sack. He ripped it aside and tarnished gold coins of every denomination appeared. As the sunlight hit the coins directly, they reflected back into Cole's eyes. He squinted and rose to his feet.

He walked over to Lady and retrieved two large heavy-duty canvas sacks. It took some time to scoop out all the coins and fill the sacks; how long he had no idea. All the while, the only thing on Cole's mind was his future with Mattie and perhaps a life of peace and tranquility. Tying the two sacks together, he slung them behind his saddle. Lady buckled slightly from the weight.

"Sorry, old girl, is it too much if I get on, too?"

In his mind, he imagined Lady said that would be fine with her. As he mounted, she did buckle again but he would go easy on the trail with her. So, with his mission achieved, they set out to return to Sudden and his new life with his love secure for the future.

A day later, Cole knew he should send word back to Mattie. She worried needlessly so he wanted to reassure her of his safety. Somewhere down this trail there was a town with a telegraph office, he just knew it. As they moved slowly along a riverbed, he whistled a tune he did not know the name of nor did he care. Life was about to become very good.

On a ridge above the riverbed, a dark figure watched Cole and Lady through a spyglass. This dark figure took note of the canvas sacks. It could only mean one thing, thought The Preacher.

Chapter   22

Cole Has an Encounter

The first town that Cole entered was Ruidoso, a known hell-hole rife with lawlessness. So much so, there was no sheriff, as too many had been killed at that civil servant job and no candidate was willing to step up for election. It was at this inopportune time of wicked lawlessness that Cole rode into this hell town with a tired Lady. Cole felt sorry for his horse. She had covered many miles and ridden hard without complaint while bearing her master on his singular trek. Next to Mattie, this blue roan was Cole's other great love.

As Lady led him along the main street of town, Cole kept a keen eye out for bushwhackers and range bums. He knew about this town and could smell its evil. The presence of a telegraph office was the sole reason Cole rode into this town at all. He could send word to Mattie of his success in locating The Saddle Ridge Horde.

Halting Lady in front of the telegraph office, he dismounted and threw Lady's left rein over the hitching rail. The two sacks of Saddle Ridge treasure, tied together by one rope, were slung over the back of his neck and tucked out of sight under his long coat. He went inside. Across the street, a figure came out from behind the blacksmith shop and watched this stranger enter the telegraph office.

A short, fat clerk with sleeve protectors greeted Cole sullenly and with disinterest. "What can I do for you, Mister?"

"I'd like to send a telegraph message to Sudden." Cole dictated a short statement to Mattie, explaining how he had found the strongbox and was headed back to her soon with its contents. He gave the fat clerk the address of The Byzantium Hotel. Now he had to get Lady a double order of oats and water over at the livery.

Two hours had passed. Cole had got himself some grub and much needed repose, time to tack up Lady and move on from this manure pit. With the two heavy sacks still slung over his shoulders, he walked down the street to the livery. Being cautious about his surroundings was second nature; he could always sense being followed or watched. That feeling came over him as he walked. Out of the corner of his left eye, a figure darted behind one of the simple shacks lining the plank sidewalk. His heavy spurs rang out on that empty street.

Suddenly, Cole sensed he was in a kind of ghost town. He knew there were people living here; he had seen several and talked with three: the fat clerk, the livery hand, and the old woman who brought his meal. Now, there was no one, just the creaking of the sidewalk planks and his clanging spurs. It was at this ghostly, quiet moment that the din of a creaky door cut through the silence. The door was thrown open to the outside of a ramshackle structure that had once been some kind of emporium, now abandoned.

Cole stopped just short of the open door as it was slammed shut. Standing before him was an odd-looking figure of a man, medium height, narrow shoulders, bit of a paunch around the waist and a wild rag tied around his face. He held a dirty Remington New Model Army .44 in his outstretched right hand. He pointed the weapon at Cole's face.

"Hold it right there ya sonofabitch!" The strange man barked.

"Ah, shit..." Cole muttered to himself. He did not like a gun pointing at him. Not one damn bit.

"Ruidoso's kinda a dangerous town, we ain't got no sheriff! Ya get yer teleegraph sent?"

"What the hell do you want?" asked Cole.

"I been watchin' you from up on the ridge outside of town. Seen you lug them sacks off yer horse. Judgin' by the way you was walkin' they must weigh quite a bit. Then, when I spied ya walkin' heavy into the teleegraph office, just knew ya had sumpin' valuable on ya. Thinkin' gold, coins, ingots, mebbe..."

"Now you wait just a damn minute." Cole did not have time for this nonsense.

"Now that's where you got it wrong, Mister. I ain't much for waitin.'"

"You don't know what the hell you're doing..." Cole said with a dark smile.

"Oh, Mister, you are wrong again! I may just be the most level-headed sonofabitch in this territory. Now kindly drop that hogleg and kick it to me so's I can admire it."

Cole took a deep breath before responding, "I don't surrender my weapon unless there is an IMMEDIATE THREAT."

The strange man cocked his brown floppy hat back with his left hand and went silent with frustration. It was obvious in his eyes as he cocked the hammer of the Remington and held the barrel closer to Cole's face. Not a smart move. "Well, then.. consider this a threat, you sonofabitch!"

It was all over in a matter of seconds. Cole reached up with his left hand, grabbing the strange man's right wrist. As he twisted, he felt the grip on the gun releasing, particularly after bones started to crunch. With his right hand, Cole pulled the Remington free, then shoved this jackass and his busted wrist into the dirt.

The man fell hard. While on the ground, he fumbled with his left hand under his belt and produced a pocket pistol.

That was all Cole needed to pass judgment as to his next move. He emptied all six chambers into the highwayman's heart. The shots echoed all over town. The blood came out in long spurts, six to be exact. Outraged by this inconvenience, he even dry-fired once more on the first spent chamber. When the heat of the moment subsided and a blood pool formed under the body, Cole tossed the Remington to the ground. He walked over the body, the hem of his long black coat brushing lightly over the huge fatal crater in the highwayman's chest. Cole was on his way to Lady and grateful to be leaving this hell hole.

God how he despised having a gun pointed at him.

Chapter 23

The Weird Loner

Cole and Lady left the abandoned mine and the town of Ruidoso far behind them. A gnawing sense of being watched or followed was never far from Cole's mind but now it was acute. As a result, they took a circuitous route back to Sudden on a little-traveled trail. As they zigzagged through the desert landscape, Cole imagined the look on Mattie's face when he returned. It was a face filled with love and hope. He was truly the luckiest man on earth. He pulled the tintype from his breast pocket and studied every detail of Mattie's beautiful visage. "Enough," he thought. "Pay attention to the road!" He pocketed the tintype.

"Come on, Lady, we have some riding left to do." He spurred her gently and she took off in a lope. They kept that pace for a mile or so until they came upon a green atoll of trees and shrubs. Must be a waterhole. They circled the clutch of trees as if it were an adversary. When Cole determined it was safe, they rode through a break.

There sat the waterhole and next to it what was left of a campfire. Next to that kneeled a man, gaunt face, ribbed pullover shirt, suspenders holding up his trousers. As he stoked the dead fire with a stick, he looked up and spotted Cole and Lady. No weapons appeared in view, just a pile of personal effects strewn over a bedroll.

"Greetings. I just doused the fire but the coffee's still hot. Want some?" The gaunt man lifted his own tin cup to his lips. "It's pretty good."

Cole slipped off his saddle, slung the canvas sacks containing his future over his shoulder and walked over to the man. "I'd be obliged," he said. "Didn't expect to run into anyone out here." Cole surveyed the rest of his surroundings.

The man poured fresh coffee into another tin cup, stood up and handed it to Cole. "Yep, not many take this trail into Sudden anymore, ever since the army cut that new pass through the hills."

Cole took a long sip of the coffee. It still was really hot. The lone man (Cole could sense he was alone) kneeled again next to the dead fire. Cole took a seat on a large rock. Nothing was said for a few minutes until Cole broke the silence. "Fact is, I'm mighty happy to see someone... anyone... out here. No horse?"

"Nope," the loner sipped his coffee. "What's in your two pokes?"

"I guess you could say our future."

The loner pondered a response. None came quickly and then: "I used to think about my future. That was some time ago. Before Martha, that was my wife, came down with the ague. Died from her fever in the back of a buckboard on the way to the doctor's office. Since then, I don't think much about the future. Just the present."

"I suppose how we conduct ourselves in the present holds the secret to our future," said Cole.

"You said a mouthful there, Slim! I guess for those of us who are alone it's one way. You said 'our future.' Referring to someone else?"

"My woman, Mattie."

The loner smiled, "Fine, spirited name."

"She's a spirited woman. Used to work a riverboat game when I met her. Finest individual with a deck of cards, man OR woman, I ever seen."

"The contents of those sacks? A ticket to your future, then?"

"Of a kind, yes. Some trouble in getting it."

The loner studied Cole, his manner, his tense, ramrod straight physique, his piercing eyes. "You've roamed much of your life?"

That was an understatement, thought Cole. "Too much," he validated the inquiry.

Another uncomfortable silence passed for several minutes.

"Be wary of easy solutions," said the loner. "Like this." He pointed at the two canvas sacks.

"What do you mean?" Cole was mesmerized by this odd man. He was bizarre yet philosophical.

"Whatever in the hell is in them sacks. If it came from an evil place, it might bring evil with it."

Cole thought about this. He had spent a lifetime facing off against evil and prevailed, but this dire warning struck him deeply. Evil had always been vanquished yet never had he possessed a thing that may be evil. "Sound advice." Cole reached into the closest sack and produced a gold coin, handing it to his campsite host.

The loner's eyes lit up. "Why, hell, Mister! That's a hunnert dollar gold piece!" He bit the coin with his teeth, tasting the solid gold. Cole swigged down the rest of his coffee and gently laid the cup down. Throwing the sacks back over his shoulders, he ambled over to Lady and threw them back on her, behind the cantle. He turned to the loner saying, "Best damn coffee I ever had." Cole pulled himself aboard Lady.

"Your peace is at hand, you can find it if you know where to look. Adios." The loner watched Cole ride through the break in the atoll, then heard his horse lunge into a trot, then a gallop. He heard this for what seemed an eternity. The loner leaned back on his bedroll, closed his eyes and dreamed of peace.

Chapter 24

Face-Off With Evil

At least six hours had passed by since Cole left the loner's camp. All the while, the man stared at the $100 gold piece as if it was but a dream. Never had he held any amount of money like this in his hands. The loner recognized something within himself he had not felt for many years. Was this hope for the future? Was it a sense of peace? Whatever, this dark stranger, though only appearing in his life for not even a half hour, had given this gift.

The loner struck a match to reignite the fire. It was time for a meal. Perhaps in the morning he would move on. The notion of rejoining society now occurred to him. As the fire crackled back to life and the flames warmed the area, the sound of jangling spurs, the Spanish variety, could be heard.

"Hallo? Who's there?" The loner looked all around him. "Is that you again, Mister?"

A figure clad in all black like a pastor, a coiled rope looped around his belted Slim Jim, appeared in the break of trees. "Easy, friend!"

The loner drew back, startled. "Jesus goddamn Christ, you scared me! Sorry, Padre..." said the loner.

The Preacher moved into the circle of the atoll. Surveying the surroundings, he looked for weapons. All he saw was the pile of personal effects, the coffee pot and the gold piece held in the loner's hand. He moved to the strange little man and stood over him.

"We live in startling times. It would appear that you had a visitor to this site," said The Preacher as he mopped his brow.

"How do you know that?"

The Preacher pointed past the circle of trees. "Tracks approaching and leaving this perimeter."

"What are you, some kind of tracker?" asked the loner.

"Only for the Truth and the Light…"

"You must be that new parson in town."

"In Sudden?" The Preacher laughed maniacally. "Noooo, nooo… although I do hope to have my own parish soon."

"How so?" The loner waited for a response but The Preacher switched the subject and seemed agitated.

"I'll ask the questions! This rider who was here earlier, tell me about him."

"Kind man. Good man, so far as I can tell."

The Preacher felt his brain squirming with frustration, "I will leave that judgment to a higher power. Now what the hell did he look like?"

"Six feet tall, dark hair, intense eyes. Serious demeanor. Say, what are you, some kind of law?"

"You can say that I AM THE LAW OF RIGHTEOUSNESS!" spat The Preacher as he leaned into the loner's face. "Do you read me, wicked one?"

Dropping the gold coin, the loner recoiled with a feeling of terror. "Say Mister, you're beginning to scare me."

The Preacher gripped the coiled rope, unspooling it, revealing a slip-knot holding the initial coil. His manner calmed as he closed in on the little man. "'Before I found the Call, I was a slave catcher before the War of Northern Aggression! Flies on the ho cake… SNAP! Then, I became a hangman. I have jerked many a bad soul to Jesus in my time. Now my purpose brings me on this holy quest to gain that fortune which is rightly mine in which I shall cleanse this land of wickedness and depravity."

The Preacher slipped the loop over the loner's neck, pulling the slipknot tightly. Bracing his right boot on the man's chest, he pulled the rope harder.

The loner gurgled an unintelligible response, his face turning red.

The Preacher was now face to face with him. "Now, tell me which way this man was riding…"

The loner pointed in a westerly direction.

"What did he tell you? Did he give you this gold piece?" The Preacher tightened the slipknot even more.

Gurgling sounds were all the loner could make as his face turned purple.

The Preacher backed off the rope tension just a bit so that the loner could actually form words again. This man knew nothing! It would be reasonable to assume that Cole would head for Sudden, given its close proximity. The Preacher tightened up on the rope and his victim started turning purple again.

The loner stopped trying to answer and started praying inside his head.

It went back and forth like this for some time. The Preacher never knew how long.

Chapter 25

A Moment of Fear

To while away the hours while her man was away, Mattie did what she did best, she played cards. This time, however, she did not play for high stakes. She played to keep her mind busy. As she sat at the big card table in the salon off the lobby of The Byzantium Hotel, she dealt to two gentlemen. They seemed fairly nice boys and they, too, were not playing for high stakes. It was as if everyone in town was doing something else to avoid thinking about that Preacher fellow.

Just then, one of the boys looked at Mattie, laying his cards face down. "Excuse me, ma'am, I think you dealt me one card too many."

"What is that?" She NEVER did that. "My apologies, we'll count it as already played. Just lay it face down to one side."

The boy did as he was told. So it went on like this. Where was her head at? She knew but did not wish to confront it. More mistakes were made on her part and she was beat three hands in a row. She laid her last losing hand face up on the table.

Both the boys asked politely if they could excuse themselves, and she agreed. It was probably a good idea. She shoved their winnings over to them and they walked away. One of them doffed his hat to Mattie as they left the gambling salon.

Down the street, somewhere, a tacky piano played "Come Where My Love Lies Dreaming." The wind howled up in a fit, blowing street dust through the double swinging doors of The Byzantium's lobby.

Mattie thought she heard a scream and ran outside to the sidewalk. As she walked a few feet, the boards beneath her button shoes creaked. First one direction, then another, as she sought the source of the scream. She stopped a passerby and inquired if he had heard it.

He assured her that other than the normal sounds of Sudden, he had heard nothing.

The piano played on and the wind howled.

Chapter 26

Reckoning

Cole and Lady approached the outskirts of Sudden, the noises of the town could be heard in the distance. A water trough sat next to the old livery stable which was hardly ever used since the new livery opened several years ago in the main part of town. In fact, the owner who lived in a shack behind the old livery was rarely seen as there was no business anymore. Everybody went to the new stables in town.

Cole slid off his saddle and guided Lady to the trough for a well-earned drink. She lapped the water furiously. Cole took off his hat, untied his wild rag and plunged his face and hands into the trough water. As he came up, he threw water on his face and the back of his neck. He used the wild rag to wipe himself dry. As he retied the rag around his neck, he closed his eyes and pictured Mattie waiting for him, ready to begin their journey to that place of peace. Everything is truly under control now, he thought.

It was at that moment Cole heard the click of the hammer of a '58 Remington. Unmistakable. Cole knew his weapons. He opened his eyes and just out the corner of his right there was the blued steel of a barrel. It grazed his temple.

"The Lord has seen fit to deliver you to me…"

Cole knew that voice. It came from the depths of depravity and the last time he heard it he wound up with several slugs in his backside. He started considering his options. He could reach for his gun, go for the knife in his boot, or fall back into his assailant and try to disarm him. All came with more risk than he cared to assume. Maybe wait for the next free moment he could get the drop on this son of a bitch.

"I shall instruct you to remove those sacks off your mount, then obey my command. Now turn around first so you may address me properly."

Cole turned around and there was The Preacher backing away, gun drawn. The sun drew down behind him splaying out rays of light from his all black frame and reflecting off the blued steel of the Remington.

Cole resisted doing anything, especially obeying this bastard's commands.

"Did you not hear me, wicked one?"

Cole moved sideways to Lady, slowly, all the while keeping eye contact with this perverted demon. Maybe he could get to his pocket gun inside the saddlebag.

"Wait," said the Preacher.

Cole stopped just a few feet short of Lady.

"I shall retrieve God's gold myself. Back off." The Preacher moved to Lady and slid the canvas sacks off her. Cole wished at that moment she was a kicker. He threw the bags towards Cole. "Now, take this fortune inside this livery. Carefully. Do it NOW!"

Cole picked up the bags. He tried to buy time. Whenever outgunned, stall, buy time, or distract. "The man that runs this place…"

The Preacher grinned like a jackal. "Do not worry about him. I sent him to the next world."

"You are a vicious bastard, I'll give you that" said Cole.

"Pick up those sacks, put them around your shoulders and raise your hands." The Preacher gestured to the door of the livery.

Very slowly, they moved inside. Inside it was dark with shafts of light beaming through partially open shutters.

"Now, drop those sacks so we may view the fortune that will be used for my holy work."

Cole dropped the sacks and lowered his right arm to do so.

"Hands up!"

Cole heard The Preacher move toward him in his heavy boots. Scanning the interior of the livery, he noticed all kinds of tack, saddles and equipment, most of it in disrepair. Above him hung rows of bridles with rusty metal bits, rings and buckles. With the right application when swung, one of these could severely hurt a man.

In a split second, Cole grabbed the closest bridle, turned and swung, making sure the bit and chain would strike first, hopefully in the face. He connected!

The Preacher screamed with pain as the bit and chain tore into the flesh of his cheek. The hit threw him sideways which caused the hand carefully gripped around the Remington to be thrown sideways as well.

In another split second, Cole reached across to his cross draw and swiftly cleared leather with his Navy Conversion. He fired and directly hit the Remington, causing it to fly from The Preacher's hand as well as provide a pretty sore nick.

"Goddamn YOU!" The Preacher lost his balance but regained it and charged Cole with all his might.

It was too close to get out another shot so Cole grabbed a pair of spurs from a stool. Wielding spurs and pistol much as a knight would use a mace and a shield, he swung several severe blows with both at The Preacher.

The howls of pain with every hit echoed in the small livery.

The idea was to get some distance and shoot the bastard.

The Preacher swung a right hook back at Cole, knocking the spurs out of his left hand.

Cole kicked at The Preacher's right boot and his own spur grazed across the leather.

The Preacher fell back into a row of dusty saddles perched on sawhorses with a loud crash. "You shall pay for this!" Quickly, The Preacher rose and charged again, pulling his Bowie knife.

Cole pulled at a wood yoke and flung it at the charging madman who dropped the knife upon the contact from yet another makeshift weapon, but he was still too close for comfort.

As The Preacher steadied himself for another run, Cole grabbed a rusted horseshoe from a workbench and hit the deranged man of God square in the head. He fell in a heap and was out like a candle.

Cole threw the horseshoe to the floor, making a loud clank as it bounced into the wall. He grabbed the Bowie and the Remington, stuffing them in his gun belt. "You got any more in you? Son of a bitch..." said Cole. He turned, grabbed the sacks and walked outside, dropping the Bowie and the Remington in the water trough.

"Need that Sheriff Duncan here," Cole said to himself. Certain this villain was out cold, he would mount Lady and ride quickly into town and alert the sheriff himself. He threw the canvas sacks onto Lady's back and led her from the old livery. He grabbed her reins and reached up to take a handful of mane to pull himself up.

They say death comes so quickly sometimes, one does not necessarily suffer. Cole felt an odd tickling sensation on his right side. A sharp, precise stab began in his lung, blasted into his stomach and then the center of his chest. Now his heart hurt. What the hell?

The Preacher gripped Cole's shoulder from behind and twisted a knife, which had been concealed in his boot. He sunk the knife in deeper and started twisting.

Blood from Cole's punctured insides gurgle up and out from his mouth. He felt weaker and weaker. What was going on? He had to get to the sheriff and then to Mattie. To Mattie, to Mattie, to Mattie...

The Preacher's brain was boiling. The hit from the horseshoe had jangled him. He was seeing double and the pain throbbed like sin, but he held the knife tightly as Cole grew limp. Pulling the knife from the lifeless body. The Preacher pushed him into the dirt.

Cole laid on the ground, face cocked sideways, blood continuing to spill from his mouth.

The Preacher wiped the blade clean with an old rag hanging from the hitching post. "God of vengeance shine forth!"

He spotted a small bell hanging by the door of the livery. He struck it with the blade of the knife and it rang out. First, The Preacher looked for his Remington and Bowie, but his head was still reeling from pain and double vision. No matter, he had plenty more weapons at his hideaway. The canvas sacks with the Saddle Ridge fortune! This was all that mattered. He grabbed them off Lady and went in the back of the livery to fetch his own mount. As he rode away from Sudden, he was still having trouble with his vision and blood was streaming from his head wound. His horse would carry him and he would recover to spread his word all through the Southwest. He spurred his mount with one bloody jab and took off in a lope.

Lady knew something was wrong. Why was her master just laying there? The sun was setting and she stood still, waiting for him to get up. Soon darkness would cover the land and not just the darkness of night. The darkness of The Preacher would soon spill out over the land as well.

Chapter 27

Doc Harrigan Brings News

The next morning, Mattie sat at a small table in her room at The Byzantium Hotel. She fiddled with a deck of cards. "Goddammit, where the hell is Cole?" she wondered to herself. The telegraph had been received days before and he sure as hell should have made it back by now.

This thought was interrupted by a knock at the door. She rose, walked across the room and opened the door to find Doc Harrigan looking glumly at her.

"Yes?"

It was then, Mattie noticed the doctor was holding Cole's hat and gun belt. "They found him... and his horse... just outside of town. Near the old livery. Miggs, the owner, was found butchered in his shack. There was also a drifter down the old road hogtied and beaten. He died this morning."

Mattie stared at the hat and gun belt in utter disbelief. The doctor handed her the items and spoke, his voice cracking. "I don't think he suffered much. He was probably dead by the time he hit the ground."

Mattie fought back the tears. This was not the way it was supposed to be. Indeed, Cole always did come back as he claimed. "Where's the damn box?"

"I'm sorry, Miss Mattie. What box? The rest of his personal effects are at Sheriff Duncan's office."

There was no "box" amongst his belongings. Mattie was both controlled yet hysterical. "He telegraphed me from Ruidoso. Said he found The Saddle Ridge gold. It was locked in an old Confederate strongbox. He looked at this as our future. I begged him not to go after it. Damn him. Damn him!" She broke into tears. The silence held between them for some time. Her tears fell onto the brim of the hat she held.

Doc Harrigan looked up from the floor. "That business with that Preacher character?"

"Yes" Mattie nodded.

"Believe me, there was no strongbox found."

Mattie stemmed her tears. She thought for a moment and then it occurred to her. "Then I know what I must do…"

"Miss Mattie, please. Enough people have been hurt in this thing."

"Yes… and it's up to me to set it right."

"If you're talking about tracking this man and bringing him to justice, I implore you to reconsider. Besides, how will you ever find this Preacher character?" asked Doc Harrigan.

"Shouldn't be difficult. He leaves dead men wherever he goes," Mattie replied.

"I urge you to reconsider. You do not know this man or his capabilities."

"Correction, Doc! He does not know what I am capable of!" Mattie slammed the door and flung the hat and gun belt on the bed. She followed. The tears streamed down the sides of her face and into the pillows. She clutched the hat close to her and cried a bit more.

Then the tears stopped. She rose up and grabbed the gun belt. The .44 was tucked tightly into the Slim Jim. She walked over to the mirror on the credenza, strapping the belt to her waist. She had to cinch it up to the last notch. She put Cole's hat on. It was a bit big for her but she could stuff a rag in the hat band. In the image in that mirror, the two of them had become one. Her mission was clear. Kill the man who had robbed her of her love, of her life.

Nothing else mattered now.

Chapter 28

An Eye for an Eye

Nobody had a clue where this "Preacher character" hid out. Most people believed him to be a myth. The law and other authorities throughout Texas and the New Mexico Territory tended to believe he existed as they investigated the crimes he allegedly committed. Still, no one had ever really seen him. Certainly anyone who had seen him wound up dead so there were no living witnesses. Yet, there were still theories, possibilities as to who this villain really was and where he resided.

Mattie thought carefully about these clues, Cole had taught her well in the deductive arts. So, she sat at the small table with a pencil and paper in her room at The Byzantium scribbling out notes, thoughts, clues, anything about this man, details that Cole had shared with her during his quest for The Saddle Ridge Horde. One thing was certain, she knew her man was lethal and he would have put up a fight in any confrontation, so this Preacher must be wounded or hurt as a result. Could he have traveled far if Cole had inflicted injuries upon him?

Mattie walked to the edge of town. She stood outside the old livery where everything had occurred.

One of the sheriff's deputies, a young man still in his teens, walked out from the shack where Miggs had been butchered. "Ma'am, this ain't no place for a nice lady to be."

"Tell me, young man, what do you know about what happened here?"

The young man with the tin deputy star thought carefully before responding. "Well, ma'am, we're not really supposed to talk about it. Sheriff says to keep a lid on it. Townsfolk might get kinda jittery."

"Tell me anyway."

"Well, that Preacher fella, he sent Mr. Miggs to his maker in his cabin. It was a real mess. Then there was that drifter who had been tortured, he was found about two miles along the old road. That pistolero who come to town a few weeks back, he laid right here, his blue roan standing next to him." The boy pointed to the ground a few feet away from the trough. Dried blood stained the the dirt.

"What are these?" Mattie pointed to some horse tracks leading away from this terrible sight.

"Sheriff says maybe they's the tracks from that Preacher fella's horse. Listen, ma'am, this ain't no place for you."

Mattie thanked the boy and walked back to town. The walk was just long enough for Mattie to devise a plan. Within an hour, she had her effects packed into her bedroll, Lady saddled, and she set out from Sudden. Cole's gun belt strapped to her waist and wearing his hat, she walked Lady to the old livery.

Sheriff Duncan stepped onto the balcony at the boarding house, watching. He had considered talking to this woman about the events surrounding her man but resisted. More so than her man, he knew she was strong-willed. Talking her out of vengeance would be useless. Another good soul was to be lost in this tragedy. He bid her a quiet goodbye.

Mattie stopped near the water trough where the dried blood sifted into the sand. She regarded the hoof prints leading away from the scene. Mounting Lady, she followed them. It had rained the day before Cole's return so the ground was soft and the tracks continued in a steady line. She followed them for miles. How many miles? She had no idea. But then, at the base of a small ridge, the tracks disappeared suddenly.

⁕

Two days passed full of fruitless wandering but Mattie persisted. Early morning on that second day, she came upon a curious character sitting by the side of the road. He wore a torn black frock coat. A bloodied right arm hung in a sling. Mattie could see he was unarmed. His eyes were like a doll's, glazed over, crazy eyes. She stopped, for what reason, she had no idea.

The man babbled incoherently and endlessly.

After a few minutes of this, she considered offering this poor soul some water from her canteen but then thought better of it. No telling what disease this wretch might be carrying.

The babbling continued and yet it appeared to have a structure to it. Was this man speaking in some unknown tongue? As the man gesticulated wildly, she spotted another wound under his frock coat.

Suddenly, he started screaming loudly.

Mattie recoiled in horror and knew she had to ride away. It was then the wretch uttered the words "preacher" and "cathedral."

She looked directly at him and he pointed to an offshoot from the main trail. He said the word "preacher" again, pointing down the side trail. After another bout of hellish screaming, the man collapsed in a heap. Mattie had no way of knowing this was one of the men Sheriff Duncan had confronted at the ambush site a few days back.

God knows how many miles she was from Sudden when she spotted the ramshackle structure on the horizon. Smoke poured from a chimney. There was something like a steeple above a double door entrance. As she rode closer she heard a voice emanating from this makeshift church. The words were unintelligible but the voice was pure evil.

Once in front of whatever this place was, Mattie dismounted. She dropped Lady's reins, grabbed a short rope from the saddle and walked to the stairs leading to the double doors. She slung the coiled rope over her left arm. The voice from Hell inside continued to bellow.

"My eyes have seen the face of God, I have touched the hem of His garment…"

Mattie slowly opened one of the doors and what she saw next, she could not believe. Inside there was row after row of empty pews, how many she could not count. Hanging from the dilapidated walls were primitive works of religious iconography, but not just the average crucifixion or resurrection paintings. These paintings were brutal and strange as if they were all composed by a lunatic child. There were scenes of burnings, sacrifices, and supernatural phenomena. They were nightmares. Mattie could hardly stand to look at them. At the head of this bizarre cathedral of evil stood several statues of a tortured Christ, John The Baptist with his severed head in his outstretched hand, a wailing Mary, and some hydra-headed beast from Hell.

Above them all in a dark pulpit stood The Preacher, wailing and ranting partly in gibberish but mostly in his own revised passages from the Old and New Testaments. He was addressing his flock who did not exist yet in his delusional madness the room was full.

Mattie walked down the aisle passing each empty pew, ignoring the revulsion and terror she felt in her heart in such a blasphemous, surreal perversion of a place of worship. She placed her right hand on the center of the gun belt, remembering Cole's advice to never show fear in adverse circumstances. As she reached the last row of empty pews, The Preacher, as if awakening from a trance, noticed her and ceased his rant.

He stared down at Mattie with those cruel eyes. Pulling his own holster and belt from the pulpit, he strapped it around his waist and descended the pulpit stair. He wore a brocaded vest with bible pages pinned to it. His head still throbbed from the beating Cole gave him, but at least his double vision was almost gone.

"At last, I find you. Here among your 'flock' as they sit in rapture over your precious words." Mattie waited for a response. It did not take long.

"Ah... dear Lord, excuse the presence in this Holy House of this harlot! Tell me, misguided lamb that you are, is it your intention to seek me out for the salvation of your soul?"

Mattie stood her ground, "I seek only one thing from you, backstabbing, back-shooting bastard that you are!"

"The only true path to salvation is through death. Did you know that, harlot?"

"I am relieved that you understand that. In this way my action here today will be justified."

The Preacher struck a perverted grin. "Why you little witch! Are you toying with me?"

"Sure, backstabber. LET'S PLAY!"

The room went eerily silent. The duo sized each other up for what seemed to Mattie an eternity.

The Preacher made the first move by sliding his right hand to draw his Remington, but Mattie drew more swiftly and cleared leather first. The report from Cole's .44 echoed like thunder in the evil cathedral.

The Preacher winced with pain and drew his right hand to his eyes discovering the cartridge had ripped clean through the palm. Blood came streaming out like a small fountain. "You Babylonian whore! I should have let you feel the edge of my Holy blade before I put it to that bastard who shared your bed!"

The Preacher reached for his Bowie knife with his left hand. Another report came from Cole's gun as Mattie blew a hole in that hand. Blood was everywhere.

Between the pain in his head and two fresh bullet wounds, The Preacher doubled over.

Mattie reholstered the .44 and grabbed the rope around her shoulder. She approached the false prophet from behind and looped the rope around his neck. Pulling hard, she dragged him to the floor.

In his pain and madness he was forced to listen.

"You see, that man was the only good man I ever knew. He may have been reckless, but he loved me. We were one person, the two of us. YOU took all that away!"

The Preacher mustered enough strength to respond, "I weep for the shootist's harlot. Your uncleanliness is in your skirts."

Mattie pulled the rope tighter.

"I presume, being a preacher, you are familiar with the Old Testament? Book Of Judges? You know the story of King Jabin and General Sisera? They broke from God and built an army of 900 chariots. But they were defeated and the prophetess Deborah predicted Sisera's death by a woman. And so for this effrontery to God, the woman Jael was sent forth to deliver justice."

Mattie looked around the room for another weapon, merely shooting this heinous villain was not good enough! It was then she spied the metal cross The Preacher often carried with him, the one with the sharp edge on the base. She pulled it from a nearby table, leaned down and whispered in The Preacher's ear, "Say hello to the devil..."

Placing the sharp end of the cross on The Preacher's temple, her boots firmly planted on the rope, she drew the .44, flipped it around backwards and pounded the cross into his head.

The scream was terrifying but it was all over in a second. The house of perverted worship was now quiet.

Mattie saw two canvas sacks at the base of the pulpit and she looked inside both of them. So this was the treasure that caused all of this. Slinging them over her shoulder, she decided to leave the rope. As she walked to the door, Mattie saw two unlit kerosene lanterns. She looked at the walls of dried out wood.

Taking the lanterns outside, she struck a match lighting both and tossed them inside. As they broke, kerosene spilled across the dried out floorboards, flames lapping up every inch of the liquid.

She mounted Lady and galloped off. Stopping after covering some distance, she turned Lady around and watched as the whole tinder box went up in flames. She hoped it would burn out all the evil as well. They made a trail back to Sudden. Where else could she go?

Chapter 29

Duncan and Brother Malice

Duncan had been riding for days in pursuit of The Preacher. With only a vague knowledge and a mere guess as to where he might be, he kept on in hope he could exercise his sworn duty. It was a complete surprise to him how close he came. There on that lonely trail, he discovered the dying Brother Malice. Shorn of that terrible frock coat, he laid beneath a tree, his wounds Duncan had inflicted days earlier had festered and the blood was caked and dried upon his remaining clothes.

Duncan pulled Buck to a stop and looked down upon him. Should he finish him off here? He pulled the drawing of the strange cathedral from his vest pocket and showed it to Malice.

"What is this and where is this?" Duncan never expected a coherent answer, his real motive was to shoot the bastard and put him out of his misery.

Malice babbled something and pointed down the offshoot road.

That's when Duncan saw the first signs of smoke in the distance.

Chapter 30

Sheriff Duncan and Mattie on the Road

Sheriff Duncan was the last person Mattie expected to find on this trail. They stopped with their horses nose to nose. In the distance, the cathedral was collapsing in a fiery blaze. Wood beams creaked as they broke, embers filled the sky.

Duncan noticed the canvas sacks on the back of her saddle but said nothing. He held up the drawing. Mattie leaned over to take a good look and he spoke, "Is that what I think it is... burning in the distance?"

"If you mean what's in that drawing, Sheriff, yes," Mattie said. "What are you doing out here?"

"It's my job. I had to find this devil... for the sake of my town, for you, and for justice."

"You are too late. He should be fried more than a grasshopper on a hot griddle right about now."

"Dead for sure?"

"Yes, Sheriff. All the evil he wrought has been purified as well."

"I might as well ride up to it, take a look-see, just to officially close the case."

"You do that, Sheriff. I have one more thing I must do." With that, Mattie gave Lady a kick and they were off.

Duncan wondered if he would ever see her again.

Chapter 31

Redemption

On the other side of Sudden, the part of town nobody rode by or through, stood an old abode church probably dating to the 1700s. An elderly Padre kneeled at the base of the church door, sweeping up glass from a broken window set in the door.

Mattie approached him so very quietly, the Padre did not even notice her presence. She spoke respectfully. "Father…"

The Padre turned around. As if to explain himself, he said "You never know where a bullet will land in this town." He rose to more properly greet her. He noticed the two heavy sacks she carried. "May I be of some assistance, young woman?"

"Say, Padre, do you have a collection box for the poor here?"

"Yes, my child, we do." It had been some time since the old Padre had collected any donations.

Mattie laid the sacks at the Padre's feet. "I want to make a donation. Your poor box goes to the poor here, not to Rome?"

"Yes, it stays here. Food and clothes to the Mescaleros. Perhaps, one day a school…"

"I'll take your word for that. There should be enough there for all of that."

The Padre kneeled down and inspected the contents of the sacks. He looked at Mattie with disbelief. "I do not know what to say."

"Just make sure it stays here and the people who need it get it. I want this fortune purified."

"Again, I do not know what to say."

"Say nothing," said Mattie as she turned and walked off.

"Young woman…" The Padre picked up the heavy sacks still in stunned disbelief.

Just then Mattie stopped and half turned, her straw-colored hair blowing in the wind, her profile reflecting in the warm sunlight. "Just one last request…"

"Yes?" The Padre set the sacks back down.

"I want you to say a special prayer."

"Whatever you ask. I will create a very special prayer in your honor."

Mattie shook her head. "No, no. Not for me. I wish it to be a prayer for the forgotten. For those who have died for nothing. A prayer for the damned."

And with that she walked off.

OTHER TALES
of the WEST

BEEN LOOKING FOR YOU

Outside the Hidalgo County line, ten miles from Lordsburg, stood Madame Myra's Palace of Pleasure. It remained the most popular house in a 100-mile radius for many years. Myra catered to all types: businessmen, cattle barons, politicians, "muy rico" types from south of the Rio Grande, as well as just average cowpokes and traveling drummers. The house had two stories with no less than fifteen bedrooms, a salon, a smoking lounge, a small bar and even a dining hall which served the finest French cuisine in ten counties. The chef was a Cantonese gentleman who formerly worked for the railroad. Some said, even if you didn't want a woman, it was worth the ride to Myra's just to eat Khan's special Fricassee de Poulet a L'Ancienne.

Myra herself was a transplant from New Orleans. No one knew why she landed here nor what she was escaping, no one cared, they all loved Myra. More importantly, they loved Myra's girls and they were available in different shapes, sizes and colors, with their rates determined personally by Myra based on each customer's poke money. In this way, Myra was a true democrat.

Marshal Julian Beckworth rode his bulky but steady Clydesdale along the path that led to Myra's. Behind him rolled a one-horse jail wagon with a driver only, no extra guard. The Marshal was just about at the end of his rope. For weeks now, he was hot on the trail of one Ned Blake, a real squirrelly type. Ned was wanted for most things from Abilene to Fort Smith, nothing severe like killing or maiming, just the usual rustling, robbery, embezzlement and a bit of counterfeiting. Of course, there were the deputies who got winged when Ned was given chase; some of them were still recuperating.

Marshal Beckworth and Blake had what some might call a "long and problematic history together." While one represented the law, the other walked the other side of that street. A number of complaints had been sworn against Ned Blake, all within the jurisdiction of Marshal Beckworth and he had just about enough of this tomfoolery. He would bring

Ned in single-handed once and for all. There might even be a hangman's noose just the collar size of Ned if the Judge was feeling up to it. After all, Beckworth had sworn to uphold the law and it was mighty embarrassing that a character like Ned, whom everybody knew was some kind of acquaintance of the Marshal's, was still at large.

The fat, heavy Clydesdale carried the Marshal to the hitching rail in front of Myra's rambling Victorian house. The jail wagon slowed a few feet behind him. Beckworth gazed up at the two story behemoth.

"I just know you're inside, you old son of a bitch," muttered Beckworth.

"You want me to go in with ya, Jules?" the wagon driver asked.

"Let me get him alone, Clem."

The big, ornately carved door swung open with a creak. Beckworth viewed the foyer from left to right and carefully walked in, closing the big door behind him. Back in town, he had picked up a few scraps of information about Ned's possible whereabouts and who he might have in his company. What was the name of that soiled dove he visited here? Lupé, that's right. Ned always did have a thing for the Mexican ladies.

Just then, a black woman dressed in practical housemaid attire entered from a swinging door. She approached Beckworth. "Sumpin' I ken help you with, Mister?"

"Yes, indeed. I will be looking for Lupé."

"She busy at the moment."

"Well, when will she be free?"

"She with Mr. Ned right now. He bought the whole day."

"Mr. Ned Blake?"

"I doesn't know his last name."

That was fine, there was a "Ned" with Lupé. It had to be him! The Marshal thought for a moment. He couldn't knock on every room, so he had to think of something right quick. Then it came to him, a trick that always works. He pulled the lapel of his coat away, revealing his badge.

The woman's eyes went saucer-like. "Oh... Miss Myra don't want no trouble in here!"

"No, no. I have some legal documents to deliver to Mr. Ned." He held up a folded copy of the arrest warrant.

"Well, I don't know what Miss Myra would say. She busy, too, right now…"

"It is very important, ma'am."

"Well, I suppose…"

"Which room?"

The woman gestured to the second room down the hall. Beckworth shot her a "much obliged" look, grabbed a chair and dragged it opposite the door of the second room. Might as well be comfortable as he would wait for Lupé the sporting lady to leave the room first. No need making a messy arrest.

Inside the second room, Lupé lay sprawled on the four-poster bed. She was naked except for a black velvet choker which Ned liked her to wear. Ned pulled his trousers up then tugged his boots on. He stood up and walked across the room to the china washbowl on the vanity table and liberally splashed water on his face. He grabbed a linen and wiped his face and neck dry, then turned to Lupé.

"Myra used to have lilac water in all the rooms. What happened?"

Lupé laughed at that statement.

"What the hell's so damn funny?"

"You are, Ned! You have the best hygiene and sartorial habits of any man I ever seen!"

"Well, what's wrong with that?"

"Nothing at all, my sweet. Come over here and kiss me."

Ned climbed on the bed and grabbed Lupé tight. He kissed her for a good solid ten minutes.

As Ned rose from the bed, he grabbed his shirt from the wall hook and put it on. Before buttoning it, he reached into his right pocket, pulling out a wad of currency. He peeled off several legal tender certificates and threw them on the bed.

Lupé blew him a kiss and then moved across the room to her pile of clothes.

Outside, Marshal Beckworth waited. That was his job, waiting. Waiting and arresting.

The door of room #2 opened quietly. Lupé looked at Beckworth quizzically. Why was this man sitting in the hallway? No matter, she had a hot bath waiting.

Inside room #2, Ned fastened his gun belt. Before he put on his hat, he checked the mirror to smooth his black hair down and straighten out anything else that needed straightening. Grabbing a thin cigar from his vest pocket, he jammed it between his teeth.

It was then that the door flew open. Ned turned and saw Beckworth, all 6'4" of him, come into the room, Colt .45 in hand. "Ah shit!" said Ned.

"Hold it right there, Ned. Freeze... just like a statue!"

Ned raised his hands and clenched the unlit cigar. "I don't want no trouble," said Ned.

"Neither do I! I've been on your trail for the better part of four months and I've lost four good men in your wake."

"They must not have been that damn good, Marshal!"

"Shut the hell up, Ned. Now kindly remove whatever iron you are currently packing... slowly."

Ned started to pull his gun with his firing hand.

"With your LEFT HAND, Ned!"

Ned switched hands and removed the pistol, throwing it on the bed. "That suit you, Marshal?"

"Yes it does. Well I'll be. A Griswold! Ain't that a bit outdated?" Beckworth carefully reached down and grabbed the discarded weapon.

"I'm sentimental."

Beckworth jammed the pistol in his belt. "Alright, you son of a bitch, turn around and face that wall... and... take it EASY." Beckworth shoved Ned into the wall, holstered his Colt and produced a pair of braces from the back of his belt. He grabbed Ned's hands and slapped the iron cuffs around his wrists, squeezing them tightly. He whirled his prisoner around facing the door. "First time I've felt safe in four months. I'll be more relieved when you're swinging from a noose in Lordsburg."

"Easy, Mr. Beckworth, I ain't been tried yet."

"A mere technicality. Start moving, tough guy," Beckworth rammed the the heel of his boot into Ned's backside.

"You know, you could let me go for old times' sake..."

"Whatever I had with you before all of this is long forgotten, now move!" Again, the heel hit Ned's backside.

They proceeded out into the hallway. The Marshal drew his Colt again and held it to Ned's shoulder. Some of the girls peeked out of the rooms to see what all the fuss was about.

Ned came to a halt, looked back at his captor and the two stood in the foyer. "Who was it that saved you from that band of hopped up Nez Perce?"

Beckworth looked at Ned with disgust. "I could square that with a Henry Clay cigar. Keep moving!"

"You've turned into a real self-righteous son of a bitch since they hung that star on you."

"Call it an epiphany."

"You never used words like that in the old days!"

"Never mind. Keep moving. Out the door, now!"

With all the noise from these two echoing through the house, Myra came out of her room and stood at the top of the stairs, looking at the captor and prisoner. "What in hell are you boys doin' making all that racket?" Myra flew down the staircase even though she wore only a bustier and a flowing silk underskirt. She stood before them. "And pullin' a gun? In MY house? Don't you know I'm upstairs with the mayor right now?"

They both looked at Myra with blank faces.

She pushed Ned aside. "Get the hell outta here, NOW! The both of you! It's bad for my business!" She turned back up the staircase.

Ned turned back to Beckworth again. "You wouldn't be doing this if Sarah was still alive."

This aroused Beckworth's ire. "Shut the hell up! I won't have you sullying her memory."

Ned paused a second or two and added, "She was with me first."

This cut dug even deeper into the Marshal. "A fact that is still entirely unbelievable to me... especially now. I'm going outside to alert Clem to open up the wagon. Those leg irons and manacles are gonna look mighty handsome on you." The Marshal headed out the front door.

Ned fumbled in the back of his gun belt with his cuffed wrists and produced a shunt key. "I'll bet that dumb bastard is still using the same key for all his braces." Ned slipped the key in the first brace and off it came. He moved his hands in front of him and removed the second. He could hear the Marshal and his wagon driver conversing. He figured he had only seconds. Pocketing the key, he laid the cuffs on a small table with a doily and an oil lamp and skedaddled down the hallway to the back door of the house, sprinting over to a covered horse pen. Lupé was holding the reins to Ned's fully tacked horse.

"Mi amor, gracias!" Ned took the reins and flopped the right one over the mane.

Lupé handed him a new nickel-plated Colt and a box of cartridges. "I figured it was time you acquired a new firearm. It won't exactly fit your holster but you can get a new one soon."

Ned took it with a gracious smile. He put the cartridges in his saddlebag. "It's beautiful but where did you get it?"

"It belongs to the Mayor. He's upstairs."

"Yeah, so I heard. You can get that hot bath now. Adios!" Ned kissed Lupé passionately and rode off.

Meanwhile, Beckworth came back inside the foyer. He yelled Ned's name aloud several times. It was then he spotted the braces lying on the white doily on the little table. He picked them up and said quietly to himself, "Ned Blake, you son of a bitch."

Lupé enjoyed her bath a bit longer that afternoon.

END OF THE LINE

Cattle towns could be lively, crowded and, sometimes, bring out the worst in men. This one was different. It was big, for sure, but had a structured peace about it. Bud leaned against a barber pole, chewing a straw and watching across the street in focused concentration. His partner and longtime friend, Luke, strolled up the sidewalk and stopped behind him.

"I didn't know where you was at," said Luke.

Bud, lost in thought, did not respond immediately. He pulled the straw from his lips and turned to his longtime friend. "Huh? What?"

"I didn't know where you was at." Luke waited another moment for a response.

"Oh, hell, sorry. Thought I told you."

"That drive boss from the Stockmen's Association is over at the hotel." Once again, Luke waited an inordinate amount of time for a response.

"So?" replied Bud with vague disinterest.

Luke was getting a bit frustrated by now. "Well, I thought that's what we came here for!"

"I'm sorry... what?"

"Them jobs, dammit!"

This rattled Bud back to reality. He turned to Luke. "Oh, hell, sure! My mind is elsewhere."

Luke looked Bud square in the eyes, "Well... let's go!"

But Bud just put the straw back in his mouth and stared across the street again.

If he didn't know any better, Luke would have thought Bud must have knocked back a few whiskeys. He was always prone to introspection while drinking.

"Did you ever think what it would take?" asked Bud.

"What? The drive to Abilene?"

Bud gestured across the street, "Ten thousand dollars a week in currency goes through that waylay station." His right index finger now pointing at some building.

"You ain't making one damn bit of sense. You been drinking?"

Bud shook his head, "Look, ten thousand dollars ships through there every week." He nodded towards The Mercantile and Railroad Exchange Bank and Trust. "You can set you Ingersoll watch by it!" Bud pointed at Luke's watch chain across his vest.

"Come on, Bud. We don't want to be late for Mr. Middleton." Luke started to make the move to walk over to the hotel but Bud stood like a statue.

"The hell with Mr. Middleton!"

"Dammit, Bud, this drive to Abilene is three months of solid, paid work. Guaranteed! Now let's go!"

"You always had all the vision of a hog lookin' for a truffle!"

"Well, hell, Bud, if we miss this one, it don't leave much for us this season."

Bud walked to the edge of the sidewalk and crouched to one knee. He became much more contemplative as he began to pull weeds from the dusty street. "Luke, you remember Colonel Ketchum?"

"I... uh... yeah sure, but that don't have no precedence over seein' Middleton for them jobs!"

Bud continued in his reflective, contemplative mood, "How he was gonna make a fortune after Jeff Davis surrendered? He had those two boys and he was gonna school them and raise them right when he bought that ferrying business…"

"So what, Bud?"

"It kept him going, inspired, alive."

"Yeah, until he caught a Minie ball in the temple one week before Appomattox! Fat lot of good all that schemin' did him. Last I heard them two boys were emptying spittoons in Tulsa!"

"Well, dammit, WE survived!"

"Now you really ain't makin' any bit of sense, Bud." Luke pulled out a small pocket knife with his right hand and a piece of wood from his back pocket with his left. He started to whittle. "Whenever you get this way, somethin' big is about to happen. I just know it!"

"Well, don't tell me we haven't kept on without some kind of hopes and dreams. We just never singled ONE out." Bud held his right index finger to his forehead.

"I well remember one time your dream was just to get home in one piece without leavin' any parts behind."

"Worst mistake I ever made!"

"What?"

"Letting you save my life, you son of a bitch. I should have known I'd never hear the end of it for decades to come."

Luke began to chuckle, "I dragged your busted up carcass all through that swamp!"

"Jesus, here we go…"

Luke whittled more aggressively, "Those boys in grey on our ass like flies on piss."

Bud closed his eyes for a moment as it all came back to him and the cannons raged in his head. He steadied himself and then rose, looking at Luke. "And you know how grateful I am."

Though the bond between the two old friends was clear, Luke continued his incredulity. "So, I give up. What's the pipe dream this time?"

"Luke, it ain't no dream in a chink opium den. That bank and exchange across the way. I've been sitting on the balcony at The Silver Slipper watching that place every day for two weeks. I even wrote down every single guard and delivery schedule."

Bud handed Luke a small leather journal from his duster pocket.

Luke read through several pages. "Looks like you got this thing clocked. But just one thing."

"Yeah?"

"Ain't we gettin' a bit long in the years for this kind of work? I can't run like I did five years ago, let alone jump a horse in mid-flight like I could ten years ago!"

Bud pointed the same index finger to his head, "It's all how you feel up here. Come on, let me show you something…"

For the next twenty minutes, the pair circled The Mercantile and Railroad Bank Exchange and Trust building. They spoke in detail about where the money shipments were unloaded, how many guards protected the money and how to neutralize them, where they could tie up their horses with a getaway hitch, what direction they would ride off and most importantly what they would do with the rest of their lives once the deed was done. Actually, they spoke the most about that. One good score like this and they could back off to a life of ease and security – if they got away with it.

Luke expressed most of the apprehension about the plan. It was, after all, a hanging offense if they weren't shot to pieces outright during the deed.

Bud assured his longtime partner they were up to the task, they had been in worse scrapes. "So that's my plan."

Luke looked at the bank then back to his partner, "Uh, well, it's pretty risky but with good timing and a bit of luck, we might just pull it off."

Bud smiled, leaned on a hitching rail and folded his arms, "You got anything better to do?"

"Other than what we come here for... no... but lemme ask you somethin'. What if we don't make it?"

"Well, then the local undertaker shoots our stiffs full of his juice and the town council charges the public two cents a head to gawk at us. When the novelty wears off, the sheriff will probably stuff us in gunny sacks and drop our remains in a hole somewhere, unless we leave a note specifying cremation." Luke winced at the proposition and shivered. Still, they had lasted all these years so far, somehow. That's when he thought better of the idea and the plan. "Might be the best thing we ever done, Bud."

"Next to that dynamite job at the old Yuma Prison!"

This caused the old partners to laugh. Then they stood by and both turned real quiet for about ten minutes.

Luke broke the silence. "That Mr. Middleton will be leavin' soon."

"I reckon."

"We ought to head over there now." Luke gestured to the hotel, but Bud stood still leaning on the rail.

"Right..."

"Well, I'll go get in line if he's still there. You comin'?"

Bud didn't move a muscle and kept on looking at the bank.

"Might as well hedge our bets," said Luke. "He might even be gone by now. At least check on it... yeah, maybe he's gone by now... or maybe he's stayin' till later... hell... but if he's gone... maybe I'll get both our names on the list, but then... ah, hell! I'm goin' to The Slipper and get me a head of steam. You could meet me there. Looks like you could use one... but then you got your plan." Luke walked off.

Bud stayed. He knew it was on.

It was to become the most talked about event within a hundred miles. Several penny dreadfuls, most of them inaccurate, were written about the robbery and they included histories of the lives of Bud and Luke, which were even more wildly inaccurate. In a way, they became heroes and part of Western folklore.

Ten years after the robbery of The Mercantile and Railroad Exchange Bank and Trust, the city fathers erected a concrete pylon in the middle of the street commemorating the event. By that time the tourist interest in the lawless days of the cattle towns was at an all-time high. The cenotaph contained images of the two longtime partners, as well as the the date and hour of their deaths during the attempted robbery.

They had been immortalized in legend. For no explicable reason, the monument was removed after standing almost ninety years. Its whereabouts, if it still exists, are unknown.

THE TAMING

The midday sun peered intermittently through the looming clouds, and the surrounding majestic mountains stood as if a fortress to the vast ranch property that covered the entire valley below. A group of various structures – houses, barns, corrals, tack rooms, feed bins, and stalls – jutted out from the center of the property. To the west, an impressive herd of cattle grazed. To the east, a crowd of people stood singing in unison, "Shall We Gather at the River." A fresh coffin sat at the bottom of a neatly dug grave. The mourners finished their singing and, one by one, walked by the grave to pay their respects. Some threw dirt or flowers into the grave, while others just walked by and wept.

Lucky Beauregard stood alone on a nearby hilltop, watching the proceedings. He had dug the grave himself not more than twelve hours earlier. Several of his hands had offered to do the job for him, but Lucky would not hear of it. It was HIS ranch, The Big MB, and it was his partner, Mike, who was now residing in that hole. Lucky felt bad that the marble marker would not arrive from the stone mason in town for another week. He took his wide Stetson off and lowered his head in solemn contemplation. At that moment, he could hear the silence of the whole valley. Suddenly, the pristine moment was interrupted.

"Lucky!" A voice shouted. It was Chauncey, the attorney at law, who was running up the side of the hilltop." I said LUCKY..."

Lucky turned his broad frame to the attorney and asked, "What the hell do you want, Chauncey?"

"Listen, this proceeding is just about wrapped up. I suggest you leave these people with some of your whiskey while you and I go over the will."

"You lawyers have no sense of decency. Can't we do that tomorrow?"

Chauncey shook his head, still winded from the run up the hill. "No dice. I'm on a train to St. Louis tomorrow. You know, that business with my brother-in-law..."

"Oh for chrissake, Chauncey. Knowing Mike's economy with words, that damn document shouldn't take long to read through. I got a pretty good notion what it says anyway." Lucky gestured towards the main house in the distance. The two men started the long walk.

⟡

In the parlor of the big house, Chauncey sat at a large oak desk, pince-nez glasses resting on his nose, holding the last will and testament of Lucky's lifelong friend. Lucky paced while Chauncey read: "I, Michael William Morgan, being of sound mind and body, do hereby bequeath the sum total of my possessions and monetary holdings in the following manner: To my business partner and lifelong friend Lucius John Beauregard, I leave all my worldly goods contained in my house located at the Big MB Ranch. Additionally, I leave him my horse, Chester."

Chauncey stopped reading and just stared at the page, clearing his throat.

"Go on!" demanded Lucky.

"Uh..."

"On with it! Not like it's a surprise anyway," barked Lucky.

"You know, Lucky, sometimes when one isn't absolutely certain of an outcome, it may be wise..."

"Just finish the goddamn thing!"

"Alright, here it goes." It was as if Chauncey did not want to read the rest. "The remainder of my estate, which includes all holdings, financial and physical, in the Big MB Ranch, inclusive but not limited to stock, horses, other animals, monetary and stock holdings, oil deposit rights, cash, and investments, I bequeath to..." Chauncey stopped abruptly.

"Well?"

Chauncey looked up at Lucky, then back down to the page. "I bequeath to my only surviving and extant kin, my sister. Abigail Katherine Morgan."

Lucky turned and raised an eyebrow, looking straight through the trembling Chauncey, who finished out the reading: "Witnessed this day, May 12, 1889, by William J. Doolin, ESQ., and Joseph Sunwalker AKA Red Eagle."

The room was deadly silent.

Chauncey said quietly, "I must confess, I didn't know Mike had a sister. You ever met this Abigail?"

"Oh yeah," responded Lucky. "Last time I saw her was almost ten years ago in Atlantic City."

"And?"

"Let's just say we never got along. A bit high-toned. Ran a garment business, as I recall. What I can't figure out is why Red Eagle never said anything about this!"

"You know how those Redskins are, Lucky, real tight-lipped."

Lucky fell back into a large leather chair. "Hell, we rode with Red Eagle for years. Can't see him clamming up about something like this."

"Well, it is a confidential matter. Who better to be a confidential witness than an Indian?"

"To hell with that, Chauncey! I don't necessarily want to contest this, but any way around it? I don't think I can work with that bitch. She hates me!"

"Lucky, as your attorney and personal friend, may I offer you some personal advice?"

Lucky nodded, yes.

"Let it go. Let this thing happen, try to make it work. If it doesn't, you can always sell your half. You really don't have any other option."

"Shit... I spent all these years building this with Mike for this to happen."

⁕⁎⁕

After several days of accepting his new reality, aided by several bottles of whiskey, Lucky ambled to his big barn to inform his ramrod of the situation. Ben was filling a feed bin when he spied his boss. "Hey Ben, can I have a few words with you?"

"Sure thing, boss." Ben closed the lid on the bin and wiped his hands. "What's the story?"

"Chauncey read me Mike's will the other day."

Ben's grizzled face turned into a broad smile. "Sure will be nice workin' just for you."

"Well, Ben, that ain't the situation..."

"What do you mean?"

"You recall Mike had a sister?"

"Not really, boss."

"Well, he does, and she's coming here. Taking Mike's place and his fifty percent."

"You shittin' me?"

"I am not."

"Well, what the hell is she gonna do here? Is she a rancher herself?"

"She ain't."

Ben thought about this for a moment and wiped his brow. "Don't know if I cotton to working for a woman."

"You'll be doing it for me, Ben."

"Whatever you need, my friend."

Meanwhile, at that moment, the harsh morning sun beat down on the stone walls of the state prison 100 miles away. The large cast-iron door rumbled slowly open, and three guards and the Warden escorted a single prisoner in shackles. The Warden kneeled down to unlock the braces restricting prisoner #347, Boone Gallagher. As the Warden rose up, he did not take his eyes off this prisoner, as all three guards had their shotguns aimed directly at him.

The Warden circled Gallagher, who cracked a sinister smile. "Saddens me to see you leave, Gallagher. The idea of you gaining your freedom is personally repulsive to me."

Boone Gallagher looked up at the harsh sunlight and back at the Warden. "Don't mince words, Warden, what do you really think?"

"You'll be back, Gallagher. You're too goddamn mean to live in polite society."

"I go my own way, bull."

The Warden handed Boone his gun and holster, as well as a canvas sack of personal effects. "Made sure you got your ticket back to my fancy hotel."

Boone checked the cylinder of the Colt and said, "It's empty!"

"Sure you will figure a way to fix that!"

"I had a horse."

"Sold him to the soap works. Enjoy your walk." The Warden and his three guards laughed.

Boone spat in front of them, "You're so crooked you could swallow nails and spit out corkscrews. So long, you bastards."

The Warden and his guards continued laughing as Boone Gallagher made his way to his newly found freedom.

Several days later, Ben stood at the railway station in town, waiting on a lady. Lucky had dispatched him to collect Mike's sister and her belongings and bring them back to the Big MB.

Through a haze of steam, the Reno pulled in on the nose of its expected arrival time. As it rolled to a stop, a dozen or more people, Ben among them, gathered at the slowing coaches to greet the arriving passengers. When at full stop, the engineer clanged the engine bell, and the travelers began to disembark.

Ben looked for a woman traveling alone, but there was no one. He waited until all the passengers had met their receptions, and now he stood alone on the platform. A dark-haired woman in a velvet dress and hat stepped off the coach. She carried a large carpet bag. There was no one else left, so Ben approached and said, "Ma'am, you must be Miss Morgan."

"Goodness, that was a very good guess," said the pretty lady in the velvet dress.

"Well, you're the only sage hen here. Ain't that big a mystery."

The woman looked curiously at Ben. "Oh, yes, I see. Is 'sage hen' a good thing?"

"Uh, yessum, sure. Let me go find the rest of your traps."

The woman pointed at the carpet bag on the platform. "That's all of it." Ben shot her a quizzical look. She added, "I prefer traveling light."

"So you do. I'm Ben, foreman and ramrod out at the MB. Been with the boys since they bought their first stock."

"Well, Ben, I am pleased to meet you. My name is Abigail, but my friends call me by my middle name, Kate."

⚜

As they rode in the buckboard away from town, not a word was uttered. Kate's carpet bag was the sole item in the payload, and it jostled to and fro as Ben hit a few rocks here and there. Ben chewed on a piece of straw and kept his glance forward. Kate could feel the tension, but after 20 minutes, Ben spat out the straw and broke the ice.

"You know Mr. Beauregard well?"

"Not well, Mr. Ben. I have not seen him in ten years."

"Well, the Big MB is one of the most lucrative spreads in ten counties."

"So I am given to understand," replied Kate dryly.

"You ain't fixin' to cause no trouble?"

Kate was slightly offended by this but did not show it. She just met the remark with silence, and then… "What trouble could I possibly create?"

"I hear stories..." With that, Ben snapped the reins, and the horses went into a trot. Nothing was said all the way back to the ranch.

⬥⬥⬥

An hour later, Lucky was signing receipts at his big desk in the parlor. Ben entered with Kate and her bag in tow.

"Hey boss, she's here. Miss Morgan." Ben dropped her carpet bag with a loud thud.

Lucky got up from his chair. He extended his right arm and walked to this woman he had been blissfully separated from for ten years. "Kate!"

She took his outstretched hand. "Well, well... Lucky... how have you been?"

Their hands slowly unclasped, and their eyes warily never left each other.

"It IS good to see you, Kate. Please sit. Ben, take her bag upstairs."

"Sure thing, boss. Just holler if you need me. I'll be out back mending the porch."

Kate sat, and Lucky walked over to the liquor cabinet. Pouring a stiff measure of whiskey for himself, he gestured to Kate, offering her a dram. She merely shook her head "no" and said nothing.

"I see you didn't come with much, Kate. Not intending on a long stay?"

"I travel light, as I told your man Ben," she said curtly. "Now, let's get down to business. I intend to make an assessment of my brother's holdings, however long that takes, so you will not be getting off that easy."

"Listen, Kate, I respect your brother's wishes, but let's just say he occasionally had some ridiculous ideas."

"So I am ridiculous, is that it?"

Lucky turned red and said, "No, no, no, Kate. Take it easy. I meant nothing by that. I fully honor Mike's wishes, and I wish to help you on what may be a hard life. You remember Mike was always such an optimist, but that's why we loved him."

"Don't patronize me! I'm here to do business."

"I was Mike's partner for the last twenty years and now I am your partner, and I wish to make it easy on you." That was a good save, he thought.

Kate could not hide her anger. "I know how you feel about me. Let it be known I have even less regard for you. For years, I wished you had never come into Mike's life. You took him from our family, put him into all kinds of questionable misadventures."

"We had a pretty good run."

"Let's do it this way – I'll stick to business and stay out of your way. You stick to your business and stay out of my way."

"You need me, Kate. I know where everything is."

"You forget that I ran a garment business back east. A very successful venture, which I've had to leave in order to sort through this cow pie."

This set Lucky off. "Now listen you..."

"You listen! I never liked you! You are coarse and full of swagger. Because of you, Mike never became the attorney he was meant to be. He wasted his time in the cavalry and those ridiculous adventures. How many times did you almost get him killed? The only reason you boys ever made any money out of any of your pipe dreams was due to Mike's good business sense."

"Kate, don't get me riled!"

"I will stay here until I am satisfied, and do not try to squeeze me out, through legal means or any other way."

"I wouldn't squeeze any part of YOU!"

"Surprising, considering your delusion as a ladies' man! Another bad habit you imparted to Mike." Kate rose from her chair and headed to the staircase. "Please show me to my room. Does this hovel have any running water?"

"Certainly! I built the piping myself."

"I need to wash my face. Hope there's no sulfur in the water."

Lucky showed Kate to her room upstairs. She opened the door abruptly, then turned towards Lucky. "I presume this door has an interior lock. I know how you are!" She slammed the door in his face, and he heard the bolt fasten.

"Goddamn you, Mike," he muttered to himself.

The next day, Lucky was in the tack room cutting leather straps when he heard someone approach on horseback. He threw down the knife and leather pieces and walked outside. It was Red Eagle, wearing a combination of Native American and cowboy apparel, astride his tallest horse.

"I was wondering when you were going to show up," said Lucky.

Red Eagle pulled tight on his reins and slid off his saddle. "I came to pay my respects."

"Why didn't you come to the funeral?"

"I was at a tribal council."

Lucky dipped into his shirt pocket and produced the makings for a couple of rolled cigarettes. "You all fixing for another uprising?"

"No, Lucky. It was a gathering for scalp training. We have a few new tricks."

Lucky rolled two cigarettes and handed one to his old friend. "I'm sure you do. Remember what Captain Patterson said when he saw you following Mike and me on a maneuver? Something about never letting a redskin get behind you with a knife."

"He was a fool. Poor commander, like most white men."

"Can't argue with you there. Never did I meet a commanding officer who looked so good with a Sioux arrow stuck in his backside." The men laughed. "Now what's all this about you witnessing Mike's last will and testament a few years back?"

"It is true."

"Well, why the hell didn't you say something?"

Red Eagle looked puzzled. "To whom?"

"To ME, goddammit... about Mike's sister."

"I figured that was Mike's business. If he wanted to tell you, he would."

Lucky paused and puffed on his cigarette. "How did we ever stand each other all those years in the army?"

"Because whenever you two geniuses became lost, I always saved your asses."

"That might have had something to do with it," offered Lucky.

Red Eagle put his hand on his friend's shoulder and gripped tightly. "How are you, my friend?"

"Fair to middlin.' I miss Mike."

"He was a good man. So are you, both men of honor."

"I just never envisioned a world without him, just as I cannot see a world without you."

Red Eagle could see Lucky fighting back the sadness. "Your soul is strong. You have the heart of a warrior. How is this woman? This Abigail Morgan..."

"She goes by Kate."

"Fair enough. We may choose our own names. I'll bet no one calls you Lucius!"

Just then, Kate strolled up behind the two friends. "May a lady join this pow-wow?" She was dressed in modest ranch-work clothes. She extended her right hand to Red Eagle. "I am Kate Morgan."

Red Eagle shook her hand. "I am Joseph Sunwalker, also known as Red Eagle of the Hunkpapa Teton Sioux."

Lucky piped in, "And betrayer of Sitting Bull!"

"Well, the food was better on your side," joked Red Eagle.

"Well, I am very pleased to make your acquaintance," added Kate. "Come with me. I will tell you brave tales of your brother. Lucky, is the redeye in the usual place in the house?"

"Of course, but had I known you were coming, I'd have locked the damn cabinet!"

Kate and Red Eagle walked off toward the main house.

<hr>

The next day, a visitor came to the Big MB in the person of the local county judge, a longtime friend to both Mike and Lucky. Judge Wilson had been their C.O. years before in the cavalry.

Ben ducked into the doorway of the parlor and spotted Lucky at his desk. "Boss, someone here to see you!" he exclaimed.

A booming voice rang out, "Attention, you insubordinate son of a bitch!"

Lucky swiveled around and said, "I stopped taking orders from you twenty years ago!"

Judge Wilson entered the room, and the two shook hands warmly.

"How's ranching life, Lucky?"

"Nothing like when Mike was around."

Judge Wilson paused and looked down. "That's why I came by, offer my condolences, and apologize for not being at the funeral. Mike was a good man."

"He will be missed. I'd do just about anything to have him back and HER gone!"

"Mike's sister? I heard about that. I remember her as a fairly comely woman."

"All I ever saw was a bossy lightskirt! Seen better tempered faces on a strychnine bottle," snapped Lucky. "Now I got her running roughshod over the property, and nothing I can do about it."

"Well, I'm sure you'll have the situation under control in jig time. Listen, there's another matter I need to talk about. Been a recent development up at the state prison. Recall Boone Gallagher?"

"Boone Gallagher? What about him?"

"He has a brother who is a highly placed lawyer with extensive political connections. Even owns a couple of newspapers. Seems this brother engineered a successful appeal case to the state court, and Gallagher received a release. I figured that since you gave the primary evidence we needed to put him away, you might want to know."

"So you figure he might come after me? Who does that anymore, Judge? This is 1896. Hard cases don't revenge or ride anymore. Hell, there ain't no more hard cases. Not like back in the day."

"You make a point, Lucky, but Boone is still a mad dog, even if he is the last one. He's also smart."

"Hell, Judge, he'll turn up dead drunk in a two-dollar cathouse most likely before he ever thinks of coming here, and if he's as smart as you claim, he will know to stay off my land."

"Just the same, it might be wise to take some extra precautions. For instance, what about this woman here now, Mike's sister?"

"Hell, I'd be grateful to Boone if he'd snatch her off the property and have his way with her. Of course, five minutes with her, and he'd throw her back like an unwanted fish. God help the man who messes with her."

"How the hell did I ever keep you in line back at Fort Sill, you disagreeable bastard?"

Lucky took a decanter of whiskey from the liquor cabinet and poured out two glasses, handing one to Judge Wilson. "I was more agreeable in those days. Cheers!"

As the days went on, nothing was ever heard about the notorious Boone Gallagher, just as Lucky predicted. Tensions heightened at the ranch. While Lucky had to admit that Kate was extremely capable, he was not accustomed to being questioned at every turn. Kate constantly reviewed the finances and was incessantly making suggestions. Sometimes new policies went into effect without Lucky's knowledge.

Whatever orders Ben received, he implemented them, no matter who issued them. Many times, Kate and Lucky would cancel each other out, leaving poor Ben to brainstorm a compromise. Still, things were somehow running efficiently. Lucky was even pleasantly surprised that the profit margin increased in just three months.

Then came that one day. At the main entrance to the Big MB, there was a road that once was a trail. Around 1895, the county did an intensive survey of all the land for the purpose of proposing new roads, or highways, as they were now termed. It was determined that where the property line for the ranch ended, at the south main gate, would be a fine place to grade for one of these new "highways."

For years, the cattle had mainly stayed within the confines of the ranch, with only an occasional stray off the main property. However, with the clearing of trees and brush and the grading of the road, more strays started to wander. The Big MB was losing five to ten a week, and Ben and his boys were constantly herding them back. That's when Kate's big idea came. Kate and Lucky rode to the south main gate and came to a stop.

"Well, Kate, what was this grand idea you had?"

"I recall a cousin of mine in Virginia had a problem with strays crossing a road a few years back. He had an interesting solution. Last night I was reading *The Stockman's Gazette,* and I came across an interesting theory. There's this thing called a cattle grid."

"A what? Never heard of one," Lucky shot back.

"Some folks call them cattle guards as well. You dig a trench the width of the crossing point of your cows and secure a metal grate over it. Cows somehow instinctively know not to cross it, and the ones that do get stuck, so they know not to do it again."

"Been doing this most of my life, and that's the damnedest thing I ever heard. You sure it'll work?"

"It's worth a try," said Kate.

On the ride back to the stalls, all Lucky thought about was how much this newfangled idea may cost.

About a week later, Lucky took the wagon into town. He pulled up to the side of the General Mercantile Store. He spent about twenty minutes inside and came out with several boxes filled to the brim with goods. Throwing them in the payload, he thought he better head over to the bank before they closed.

It was then that he heard a voice from his past. "Well, well, howdy-do, Mr. Beauregard."

Lucky swung around and looked straight into the crazy eyes of Boone Gallagher. Four hard cases followed behind him.

"What's the matter, Mr. Beauregard? You don't remember me?"

Lucky eyed all five of them. Damned if this was the one time he went to town with nothing but a small pocket Colt. "What do you want, Boone?"

"Well, sir, I ain't made up my mind yet about that. The years in that prison gave me all kinds of ideas. Started thinkin' that you had a lot to do with me goin' to that place."

"I guess you should have thought about that before you stashed stolen army rifles on our property."

"Also heard you're doin' REAL WELL on the MB."

"What of it?"

Boone doffed his hat and held it up against the sun. "Well, sir, you know how hard it is to secure decent employment after a stretch, so I was thinkin' you just might want to help me get reformed into polite society. I did get a pardon, after all."

"The only reforming you'll do, Boone, is finding different ways to steal."

"So you just gonna brush me off?"

"You all are wasting my time!" Lucky turned his back to them and walked down the street to the bank.

"That'll be the last time you show me your backside, Mr. Beauregard." Boone was actually smart enough not to start anything in town.

⚬⚬⚬⚬⚬⚬⚬

It was getting well into the evening. Lucky sat in front of the fireplace, sipping some cognac, and thinking about his confrontation with Boone and his boys several days ago.

Kate walked into the room. "Lucky, I'm sending Ben and some of the boys into town tomorrow to pick up several rolls of barbed wire. The wire on the north side is just about rusted through."

"Funny thing, Kate, I remember when wire was the first sign that civilization hit the territory. Mike and I avoided using it for years."

"Well, you two old timers were set in your ways."

"Been thinking a lot about the ranch and how things are now."

"Times change, Lucky. You have to change with them."

"What I mean is, I may have been wrong about you."

Kate sat down in the chair next to Lucky and replied, "And I may have been wrong about you. You are still hardheaded."

"Have a drink, Kate." Lucky poured a generous helping of cognac into a crystal glass.

Kate took her first sip. "Mmmm. Brandy. Haven't had any since my cousin's wedding."

"So how is it you never married, Kate?"

Kate looked down at her glass. "Reckon I never had time, what with the business and all." She drained the glass, and Lucky reached over and poured more. Kate started to cry.

"This will help," Lucky said as he held up the bottle. "Now what's all this, Kate?"

"I never really grieved for my brother, and I guess it is hitting me now. You know, I never saw him much for years, and I blamed you for that. Now, after all these months here, I have come to understand what his life really was and how you made that life possible for him. I admit I was wrong about you. Do you understand?" She looked up at him, tears welling in her blue eyes, her raven-colored hair obscuring her right cheek.

"My God, Kate."

"What? You think I am silly."

"No, I think you are beautiful. You know what Mike was to me, how important he was."

"Yes, I know. You two were inseparable. Maybe that is why neither of you two ever married. That and all those women of yours!"

"Kate, I figured my time for marriage was left way in my past, and I reasoned I never had the time either, what with the ranch and all."

At that moment, something clicked. Both of them felt something they had never felt before and certainly never anticipated from each other. Kate leaned into Lucky's chair. He leaned into her. For a moment, they just looked at each other with an inch between them. Then Kate planted him with a full kiss, which seemed like a beautiful eternity.

She pulled back. "Didn't expect that, cowboy!"

Kate left her own chair and landed on his lap. They kissed again. This time her arms were fully embracing him, and he held her tightly to him.

"Too bad you're so damn old," she said with a laugh.

"Not much older than you, my dear." He rose from the chair, with Kate still holding on. Grab the bottle, I'll show you how old I am!"

With that, he carried her up the staircase. Kate held the bottle. The door to Lucky's bedroom slammed shut. Neither of them left that room all night.

⁂

As morning light streamed through the bedroom window, somehow Kate knew they had slept late. She heard the wall clock downstairs chime eight times. She rose from the bed and tried to find her clothes, which were strewn all over the floor. She looked out the window and saw the buckboard was gone, which meant Ben and some of the boys had set off to town.

Lucky rose from the bed and looked at her in a way he had never looked at her before.

"Looks like we got the place to ourselves, cowboy."

Lucky smiled and said, "Until Red Eagle comes back from his deer hunt. He'll probably come in through the north side."

"Well, let's make the most of our time, Mr. Beauregard." She jumped back on the bed, and they started to get busy when suddenly a strange voice shouted from outside the house.

"Hello there! In the big house!"

"What the hell?" Lucky got up and pulled his drawers on. He looked out the window and saw a sight he did not want to see. It was Boone Gallagher. Just then the bedroom door burst open, and two of Boone's hard cases came through, guns drawn.

"Well, lookee here. Shacked up with a pretty-painted lady. Get dressed, the both of you."

Moments later, a stunned Kate and an angry Lucky stood on the porch of the house, facing Boone Gallagher. Both had their hands tied behind their backs.

Gallagher addressed his two boys, "You two go help the other two with them cows, NOW!" Then he turned his attention to Lucky and Kate.

"Well, this meet-up is more to my liking, Mr. Beauregard. I see your hands are all gone. That's just fine. See, the boys and me will be taking the lion's share of your stock. We don't need extra hands interfering, though the boys may be disappointed, as I promised them there'd be some shooting today. Maybe there will be, just the same. Seem to recall you had a partner, tall sonofabitch like you. Where's he at?"

"He died," responded Lucky.

"And who's this filly?"

"She's my new partner."

"Well, ain't that cozy? Seems you improved your partnership. Sure she gives out benefits your old one didn't. Kinda fancy her myself. Though not sure what she sees in an old timer like you."

Kate spat, "He's ten times the man you'll ever be, lowlife!"

"Woman has sass!" With that Boone walked up and slapped Kate across the face.

Lucky turned and tried to headbutt Boone, but he missed, and Boone connected with a shot to his stomach and then a left hook to Lucky's right cheek. He kept beating on him, with Kate screaming to leave him alone, until he fell back, bruised and bloodied.

Boone's boys had started to move most of the cattle in the direction of the main gate. The only two remaining ranch hands came running out of the barn and saw four men on horseback herding the cattle. They were shot out of hand by the gunmen.

"They weren't armed," said Lucky as he spat blood.

Well, I did promise the boys some shooting today. Now, I am inclined to shoot you as well, Mr. Beauregard, and take this little filly here for fun and games, but I do have my scruples. I reason that financial ruin is good enough for you to pay your debt to me. Hope never to see you again."

Boone hopped on his horse and rode out to meet his boys and the rapidly speeding herd headed for the main gate.

"Seems you need me to save you again, paleface!" It was Red Eagle, who came out the front door. He pulled out a large knife and cut the bound hands of Kate and Lucky free. "Came in the back door, was leaving you some venison from my hunting trip, and I heard the shooting. Thought you could use some help."

Red Eagle drew an arrow from the quiver strapped to his back and pulled it tightly across his bow. One of Boone's men was the recipient, and he fell to the ground. Another arrow let loose hit a second man, who went down.

Boone had a confused look on his face. Still, the herd charged.

Kate threw open a large chest on the porch and removed a Winchester, which she tossed to Lucky, and a scatter gun, which she cocked. The three walked down the steps of the porch toward the running heard.

Then something odd happened. The entire herd just piled into each other at a dead stop. Boone was whooping at the cattle to spur them on.

Red Eagle aimed another arrow and hit his third target through the neck.

Lucky fired his Winchester and brought down the last man. Kate readied the scattergun, but Lucky claimed Boone belonged to him and the scattergun might hit some of the animals. He fired, hitting Boone in the right thigh, and he went down.

Kate's cattle grid had worked and brought the lead cows to a dead stop. The three approached what was left of Boone's gang. Only Boone was left alive. Kate pointed the scattergun directly at him.

"No, Kate. He's going straight back to prison, although cattle rustling may still be a hanging offense in these modern times. Hopefully it is."

⚜

The wedding party stood next to Mike's grave. He had a right to attend, as it was his sister marrying Lucky. Judge Wilson performed the ceremony. Red Eagle stood next to his old friend in full Sioux dress. Kate wore a cream-colored gown and never looked lovelier.

"Do you Lucius Beauregard..."

Lucky interrupted, "Don't ever call me Lucius, Judge!" He looked at Kate. "And that goes for you, too."

"Do you Lucky take..."

So the vows were taken, and Lucky and Kate lived the rest of their lives together, with brother Mike always in their thoughts. Lucky even had a portrait made from a tintype of Mike, which hung in the parlor for the rest of their days.

Kate sold the garment business because ranching was now in her blood.

Judge Wilson made sure that cattle rustling was still a hanging offense, and Boone was stretched at the end of a rope.

The cattle grid or guard received its first patent in 1915, with no credit to Kate.

152

DAY OF RECKONING

Somewhere in Kansas during the final days of the Great Conflict, there was a lone farmhouse. The property had long been abandoned and weeds sprouted where crops once thrived. The land was of no strategic value to the Union or the Confederacy yet there were both armies pitted against each other. Actually, a confused and retreating Confederate Army was shelling what they thought was a concentration of Union forces, but in reality was only three men who wore the blue. These three men were hiding in the lone farmhouse as the Confederate cannons roared.

Inside the dilapidated farmhouse one man, a Captain, paced back and forth while two enlisted men crouched on the floor, clutching their Springfield rifles. The Captain peered out the window as the cannonade continued.

"They haven't touched us yet," said the Captain.

The other two men, a Sergeant and a Corporal, looked at each other. The Sergeant rose to address the Captain. "Sir... when the hell can we leave this deathtrap?"

The Corporal leaned his rifle against the wall and looked at the Captain. "Yeah, Captain, why are we waitin' to get ourselves all blowed up? Johnny Reb has the field. The rest of the company is over that ridge. Can't we just skedaddle?"

The Captain turned from the window, his face obscured from shadows in the half-light of the room.

"There will be no desertion on my watch!"

"Not talkin' desertion, Captain" said the Sergeant. "We can take THAT with us." He pointed at a locked wooden strongbox with military markings and a federal government badge.

"Sergeant, that is your only purpose in life right now – the security of that damn box and its contents."

"Ah, come on, Captain," replied the Corporal, "if that cannon barrage gets any closer, we're gonna be layin' right under it. What'cha say we take the strongbox and hold up over the ridge?"

The Sergeant spoke next. "He may be right, Captain. One ball can blow this tinder box to all hell."

The men had a solid point but that didn't change the situation. "My orders are to stay here until the column arrives... which I judge should be shortly."

"Sounds like deliberate suicide to me..." shrugged the Sergeant.

"I will not speak of it again!" shouted the Captain. Outside the cannon barrage crept closer to the house. The concussion of the fragmented cannon balls now shook the framework of the farmhouse. Bits of ceiling tumbled down inside; it felt like a rattling earthquake each time.

The Sergeant and the Corporal stepped away from the Captain and huddled in a corner.

"Are you thinking what I'm thinking?" the Sergeant asked the Corporal.

"Runnin'?"

"Not exactly running... just relocating."

With that a Confederate cannon drew a direct hit on the house, smashing part of the roof in and destroying a wall like a pile of matchsticks. The noise was deafening. Smoke and cinders flew about the room. As the debris settled, the Captain lay on the floor, struck on the head. He was either unconscious or dead. The cannonade continued more loudly than before.

With his ears still ringing, the Sergeant swept the dust off his face and sleeves with a glove. He turned to the Corporal. "You alright?"

"Yeah, I think so. A bit stunned." The Corporal spit some dust out.

"Now's our chance."

"For what? asked the Corporal.

"To get the hell out of here!"

"What about him?" The Corporal pointed to the Captain who began to stir.

"The way I see it, the Rebs will have this field in the next hour. This house will be blown all to hell. There won't be anything left... including witnesses."

The Corporal looked at his Sergeant not believing they were contemplating desertion. "And we skedaddle up the ridge until the rest of the company arrives?"

The Sergeant nodded.

"So no one will be the wiser?"

A second nod.

"And we don't have to tell no one nuthin'?"

Another nod.

"Jes' mebbe the house got blown to all hell but we got out?"

Another nod.

"Then what're we waitin' for? I ain't gettin' under a cannonball with them Rebs so close to surrenderin'!"

The two packed up their gear and headed to the door. The Sergeant stopped and turned. "Aren't you forgetting something?" He pointed at the strongbox. "THAT!"

"Might take two of us to carry, Sarge."

"It's filled with paper, fool! Government issued legal tender. I'll take the gear, you handle that."

The two men fled what was left of the house and zig-zagged up the ridge, all the while hoping they would avoid a cannon hit. After what seemed an eternity, they hunkered down at the top of the ridge and looked down. The barrage now struck the rest of the house and it collapsed in an ear-shattering explosion. Fire leapt from the piles of collapsed wood.

"Damn, must have been some combustibles in there!"

The Corporal looked a little concerned, "We just left him there."

"Tragedy occurs in war," said the Sergeant coldly. "Come on, let's go."

The Corporal sat upon the strongbox. "What we gonna do with this thing?"

"We are going to hide it."

"Good idea, Sarge, keep it outta reach from them Rebs. When the column comes back, we just tell 'em where it's at. Might get a medal for savin' it!"

"I'm not telling them anything, my friend."

The Corporal was slow on the uptake as he looked quizzically back.

"You see, it never made it out of that house. Look at those flames! Burned right through the wood and all the paper inside went up with it."

The Corporal got it now, he nodded with a smile.

The Sergeant put one hand on the Corporal's shoulder and looked him directly in the eye. "Let me tell you how this box is going to change our lives…"

Many years passed and the world changed. People changed. The West changed. Some changes were good, some were not so good. A formerly lawless land was tamed into lawful order. Business was good.

Inside a well-appointed government office, a mechanical wall clock ticked loudly, the only sound in the room. At a large mahogany desk sat Nathan "Bully" Brown, Lt. Governor of the Territory of New Mexico. He faced a mountain of documents which he signed with a mechanical timing matching the wall clock. A knock on the door interrupted this routine.

"Come."

A nattily dressed bureaucrat entered the office. "This letter just came for you, sir."

Nathan "Bully" Brown looked up from his paperwork. "Leave it on the desk."

The bureaucrat dropped the letter, turned, and left the office. Nothing else was said. Bully dropped his pen, accidentally hitting the inkwell, spilling some of the black ink on one of the documents. It spread like a bloodstain.

"Dammit."

Bully rubbed his aching forehead, stood up, and grabbed the letter. He walked over to the light of the big bay window and slit the letter open with an index finger. He put on his spectacles and read its contents. Had anyone else been in this room they would have witnessed Bully turn white with fear.

❧∾⧙◈⧘∾❧

Many miles away, a lone figure stood looking down at a large mining operation. The roar of blasting powder and steam from mechanical shovels permeated the air. Above the noises of excavation were the voices of men shouting orders. A work whistle blew for the next shift of miners to take their place.

The lone man in a tweed suit and a bowler hat chewed on an unlit cigar. He was proud of what he saw as he built it all with his own hands and gumption. Cassius M. "Cash" Hughes was pleased with himself, that's for sure, and pleased with the politicians whom he got elected in this territory who in turn helped him.

A miner in overalls, covered in soot, ran up to this man of greatness. "Mr. Hughes, the payroll just come in!"

"Cash" Hughes turned his attention to the miner as Moses would look upon the Children Of Israel. "Thanks, son. I'll be right in to count it."

"Oh... and this came for you." The miner reached in a pocket and produced a letter, handing it to Hughes.

"Very good. Best be off. New shift comes in."

The man nodded and ran off.

Hughes reached into his vest pocket and pulled out a small knife, flipped it open and cut the envelope along the seam. As he read a strange feeling came over him. Many years ago, "Cash" Hughes had learned never to show fear. This was the surest way to success. It was everything he could do not to reveal to the hundreds of men in that mine pit what he felt deep within him upon reading the contents of that letter.

The streets of Santa Fe were bustling. People moved to and fro going about their business with precise purpose. Into this order rode a figure clad in black upon a pale horse. The Stranger rode to what appeared to be the busiest saloon in town, an elaborately decorated establishment named The Lost Love. He tied his horse and went inside, found a table and ordered a bottle.

Across the bar room, two gentlemen in expensive suits spied this alien to their fair city. After some whispering to each other, they proceeded over to the newly-arrived visitor's table.

The Stranger was focused on a leather-bound book. A bottle of tequila and a glass stood at the ready. He took a good, long, satisfying sip.

"Afternoon! Welcome to our fair little city. One of the most modern west of Abilene," said the first man to the Stranger. The second man chimed in and the Stranger closed his book and looked up.

"Indeed, what my colleague speaks is the truth. We have all the latest conveniences here, even an electrified elevator over at the Hotel Francisco! As Deputy Mayor I am obliged to help all newcomers. How may we direct you in our hamlet?"

The Stranger looked at these two jaspers like unwelcome relatives. "I am familiar with your town. I was here as a young man, during the late conflict between the States. I am sure much has changed but I can manage on my own. Muchas gracias."

The Stranger went back to his book and his tequila. The first man continued with the banal conversation. "Well, frankly, we don't see many travelers of your type through here much anymore."

The Stranger closed his book again and looked up with some consternation, "What would be 'my type'?"

"I'd say you were some kind of road agent or maybe a lawman by the looks of that hogleg tied to your side."

"I'm neither," said the Stranger.

The second man chimed in. "Fact is, Mister, we have a policy to leave all firearms off one's person while in town."

"Sounds dangerous," leveled the Stranger.

"We call it civilized. So what brings you here?"

"My name is Calder."

"Just trying to be neighborly, Mr. Calder. I am Deputy Mayor Lester Hannaday and this is Gus Strode, Accounts Manager at the Hughes Mining Company." He pointed at the other man.

Calder showed no interest. "That's nice."

"Are you looking for work, Mr. Calder? Plenty of jobs to be had here in town."

"Not really interested," replied Calder.

The Deputy mayor sensed the tension. "You'll find this part of the country has changed. Not much need for you 'pistoleros' anymore. You probably wouldn't know that as its been some time since your last visit with us."

"I am a teacher of philosophy, actually..." said Calder coldly.

"A man of letters. Why look, Lester... *Plato's Ethics*... ha!" Strode said with false enthusiasm.

"Gentlemen, may I enjoy my tequila?" That more or less ended Calder's introduction to the new, modern Santa Fe.

⸻⸻

Several miles outside of Santa Fe, at a private dining salon located within a very exclusive gentlemen's hunting lodge, sat Nathan Brown and Cassius Hughes. They dined upon quail eggs, fresh trout and a large roast breast of pork. French champagne gently washed it all down. Fine dining was not their purpose, however; it was to sort out what could be a potential problem for both of their livelihoods.

"We must get to the source of this!" cried Hughes.

"Easy, Cash, I don't think we have a problem," replied Brown as he chewed a large chunk of roast pork.

"Hannaday and Strode both reported a visitor to town who in the old days would have been labeled a 'shootist.' It could be related."

"As I said, easy there, Cash. What makes you think this stranger has anything to do with the two letters?"

"I have spent a lifetime being cautious! It has always paid off. Covered your ass during some of your sloppier moments." Hughes was direct and utterly serious while thinking Brown to be careless.

Brown became furious, throwing down his empty fork. "It was my connections that got the both of us to where we are!"

"Maybe so... but it was my brains. I remember a time when you couldn't even speak properly."

"Now, Cash, you know I suffered an impediment. Elocution lessons fixed that!"

"But not your limited brainpan..." replied Hughes.

Brown could not respond, as he knew the truth.

Many years back, Hughes and Brown had mustered out of the army with seemingly nothing to go on except their mutual secret. For the next couple of decades, their fortunes and fate were inextricably linked. Brown hailed from a well-placed family. Afflicted with a stammer and slightly dull-witted, he nevertheless found success in territorial politics with thanks to his family's connections. His political career had been bankrolled by Hughes from a mysterious source of financing. Hughes had been raised in an orphanage and remained bitter about it throughout his years. While Brown definitely pulled political strings, it was Hughes who was the master strategist behind their trajectory to fortune and power.

With the receipt of these two strange letters, it was agreed by both men to bring on some extra insurance in the form of an enforcer or bodyguard. Hughes spearheaded this, of course, and contacted a former Pinkerton agent he was acquainted with some years back. The answer to this request came in the form of Calder, a fact that Hannaday and Strode were unaware of upon meeting him in The Lost Love.

Calder met with Hughes and Brown at the mining offices.

"Do you understand our problem?" Hughes asked Calder.

"I might have a better understanding if I viewed the contents of those two letters."

"That's our business. We've given you enough information and you are being handsomely paid!" bellowed Hughes.

Calder paused before addressing the two men. "Then let me get this straight. You two gentlemen have been threatened in some vague way and I am to watch your backs. Is that about the size of it?"

"Exactly," replied Brown.

"Well, if I am to provide security, I will need to study your work routines and your daily schedules."

"You shall have our complete cooperation," said Hughes.

There was something about Calder that both men noticed right away. He seemed to exude a strange light around him and his face was roughly hewn by what appeared to be scars long ago healed. He was definitely menacing, which was what they needed.

And so the days went by and Calder watched and waited. No signs of threat or danger appeared. Calder stood by and drew his pay.

Then one day, there was something to see. While waiting at Brown's home, Calder heard a scuffle down the hallway. A woman emerged, her dress torn and a bit of blood on her lower lip. She looked at Calder and ran up the stairway.

Brown followed and stopped in front of Calder.

"She went upstairs."

"You just forget all about her," muttered Brown as he left the house.

The woman came back downstairs when she was assured Brown had left.

Calder handed her a hot cup of tea.

"Thank you. My name is Ellie. Who are you?"

"Name's Calder."

"Who are you around here?"

"Just one of the hired hands."

Ellie noticed a strange light around this roughly hewn yet vaguely handsome man. There was something about him, dangerous but with kind eyes. She was used to being around dangerous men her whole life, but this one she was not frightened by. She even sensed feeling safe and protected.

"What do you do, hired hand?" asked Ellie.

"Helping Brown and Hughes with a security issue."

"I see." Ellie could not take her eyes off this Stranger.

"Do you live here?" Calder inquired.

"No. Bully puts me up in a small house nearby."

"Are you his wife?"

"Men like Brown and Hughes do not have the luxury of marriage with their hectic responsibilities. Although Bully was married once. Don't know what happened. Hear tell she disappeared. Thank you for fetching me the tea."

Later that afternoon, while counting payroll in the mining office, a bullet pierced the window and flew into the wall missing Hughes by inches. Calder was summoned. He checked the perimeter and interviewed several of the miners who all claimed they neither saw nor heard anything.

"It may be wise for you gentlemen to lay low for a while," said Calder.

"I have a business to run! Who the hell is gonna run it if I'm not here?"

"You hired me, Mr. Hughes. That is my recommendation."

"Well, it's clear to me I am the prime target. I shall require you to be my shadow for the time being."

Several days later, there was a small explosion at "Bully" Brown's house. Calder and Hughes arrived while a group of laborers cleaned up the mess.

"Who has access to the explosives at your mine, Mr. Hughes?" asked Calder.

"All the nitro and dynamite is kept in a locked cage. Takes two keys to open it, of which I solely possess the second key."

"No other copies?"

"None. We keep a record of all explosives removed and their purpose noted."

Brown just stood there looking very worried.

"I advise you to check the inventory. Obviously, your security system has been breached."

"Ride back to the mines," said Hughes. "See the foreman and check on that. What makes you so sure the explosives came from my operation?"

"Just an assumption. I believe any threat you gentlemen have comes from within."

Calder mounted his horse and rode off.

Hughes turned to Brown and shook his head. "This is all mighty strange. Anybody see anything?"

Brown shook his head. What he did not confess was that there was something missing, a locked document box containing compromising information.

<hr>

Several hours later one of the house servants returned from the smokehouse with a slab of bacon and an empty tin box which had been shot open at the hasp lock. The aged negro dropped the bacon slab in the kitchen and brought the empty tin to Brown and Hughes, who sat in the parlor drinking whiskey.

"Found dis behind de smokehouse, Mistah Brown…"

Hughes inspected the mangled document tin.

Brown knew exactly what it was but said nothing.

"What the hell is this?"

"Ah, nothing, Cash. Probably just some junk one of the hands left behind," Brown lied.

"Something you're not telling me, Bully?"

"Forget it, Cash…"

The next day, Calder reported to his two employers that the explosives had indeed come from the mining operation inventory and, of course, no one had seen anything.

"What the hell, did it just materialize itself out of the lock up cage? Without my secondary key, access is impossible!" Hughes wrinkled his brow as he bellowed.

"One of your assistants identified a missing case of dynamite, which had been stacked neatly on a numbered shelf. The number corresponded to the inventory list indicating that slot had recently been stocked with a fresh case."

"And no signs of forced entry?"

"None, Mr. Hughes…"

"So that means some son of a bitch has my dynamite!"

"It would appear that way…"

Just then, there was heard a loud rumble followed by cries from many men. Brown, Hughes and Calder went outside to see what was going on.

One of the miners, his face bloodied and his carbide lamp broken, shouted from the pit. "Mr. Hughes... cave-in... main tunnel!"

Hughes wrinkled his brow again. He turned to Calder. "Seems we've had nothing but chaos and havoc since the day you showed up."

Calder stood his ground. "Perhaps you should look inward as to the source of your troubles. I suggested that before."

"We will deal with all this later..." said Hughes. "Right now I have a larger crisis on my hands."

Back in town, the editor of the *Tribune Express* showed up at the Lt. Governor's office. He asked the secretary if he could get an audience with Mr. Brown. The officious secretary looked up from his endless paperwork and dryly replied that the Lt. Governor was elsewhere on business. Thus, the editor of the *Tribune Express* was left alone to ponder the meaning of the rather interesting and damning documents which had mysteriously arrived at the newspaper offices.

Hughes had sent a dozen men into the main shaft to begin the process of shoring up the collapsed timbers. At least six men were unaccounted for and two dead were pulled from the cave-in. This couldn't be an accident, thought Hughes.

Daylight was ending and the men had made little progress. Hughes quickly convened a meeting with his best engineers. There was a possibility that by approaching the cave-in from a different tunnel, the men might have greater success. Hughes understood this and agreed. Brown did nothing.

"Very good. We approach it from shaft number three. Steam-driven lift in that shaft; we can haul the shoring timbers more quickly. Worth a try." Hughes ordered the men to begin organizing all the necessary equipment around shaft number three. What had not been considered was the unstable condition of this shaft, which was why it was rarely used. Maintenance had been minimal over the years. Nevertheless, the men began to organize while Hughes and Brown moved to an observation platform near the mouth of shaft number three.

"You still here?" Hughes asked Brown.

"Look, I got my investment in this operation, too."

The men began loading equipment onto the lift. Calder approached the two men who now spoke to each other in hushed tones while eyeing Calder. He noticed an ax, a pick, a shovel, and a sawed-off shotgun fixed to a rack on the platform, as he drew nearer to Hughes and Brown.

"Does it sometimes feel as if the whole world is crashing down?"

Hughes and Brown stared back at Calder pondering this strange question. "What the hell does that mean?"

"It means this might be the end of the line. You see, there was once a strongbox containing Federal Government notes. In official reports, it was blown up under a Confederate barrage. But it wasn't."

"Cash, what's he sayin'?"

"Allow me to further elaborate. This small fortune was used to build a political and business empire in the territory. Certain payoffs were made to the right connections over the years and power was solidified. I find the most fascinating part is that this whole mining operation is built on government land, tribal land to be exact. Of course, the falsified land contracts no longer indicate that. Should be interesting when the territorial and federal authorities find this out."

"What are you implying?" asked Hughes.

"Not implying anything, just stating the facts."

"You have no proof..." said Brown.

"Don't I? Well it's a good thing the editor of the *Tribune Express* has all those detailed documents from that formerly locked tin box."

"Documents? Documents? You dumb son of a bitch, Bully, did you retain documents?"

Brown couldn't answer as he was too afraid. Afraid not of the accusation, but afraid as he recognized Calder for the first time. He turned white.

"The next time you leave a man for dead, make sure he's dead!" Calder's face turned menacing. The hints of the facial scars became more obvious.

"Why you bastard..." Hughes grabbed the sawed-off shotgun from the rack and cocked back the hammer, but not before Calder cleared leather with his Single Action Army, firing at Hughes' wrist holding the shotgun. As Hughes winced with pain, his arm flailed downward and he hit the trigger, blasting a huge hole in the observation platform that blew clean through to the number three shaft. Both men tumbled down to the bottom shaft, hitting the floor stunned and bleeding.

Meanwhile, the steam lift was now fully laden with men and material. One of the men saw Calder and asked, "Can you let us down, Mister?" Evidently, they had not been aware of the shotgun blast as they were so focused on their duties.

Calder walked over to the lever and pulled it. Steam shot from the engine and the lift went down. The crushed bodies of Hughes and Brown were not discovered until the lift returned the men to the surface the next morning.

Near the scene, some days later, one of the miners found a book. It was a philosophy book. One passage had been underlined – "Justice is the quality of the soul." Seemed a bunch of gobbledygook so he tossed the volume into shaft number three.

The crimes and double dealings of "Bully" Brown and "Cash" Hughes made all the papers from Santa Fe to Boston. Eventually, a dime novel would be written which sold well for a few years. The tribal lands including the mining operation reverted back to the Pueblo Tribe.

Calder was never seen again in Santa Fe. He was never seen again anywhere. No one was ever sure where he came from or what happened to him. There was one thing. He was seen riding out of town with Ellie.

AFTERWORD

The main story in this volume is based on my original screenplay of my first produced feature. The additional stories are from ideas which might have been other possible screenplays. Who knows, maybe one day they will be. I would like to thank and acknowledge several important people who have helped me on this journey resulting in my first book.

First, I wish to thank Craig Hamann for his help in pulling this project together. Craig is a fine writer himself and has penned three of the most recent films I have directed. Multiple cheers to Curt Lambert and Buddy Clements for all those joyous times on and off set and in that special acting class. A nod of gratitude goes to my business partner and co-star in several films, Alexander Nevsky. It was Alexander who suggested I take on this project.

Lastly, I would like to acknowledge the influence of the great Clu Gulager without whom I never would have chased this dream I am living right now. My life is richer for having called these gentlemen my friends.

Joe Cornet

ALSO BY JOE CORNET

PROMISE (with Elle Marlow, 2021)

FILMS DIRECTED BY JOE CORNET

TAKEN FROM RIO BRAVO (2024)
(also executive producer)

NIGHT OF THE CAREGIVER (2023)
(also executive producer)

GUNFIGHT AT RIO BRAVO (2023)
(also executive producer)

PROMISE (2021)
(also producer)

INCIDENT AT GUILT RIDGE (2020)
(also producer)

A PRAYER FOR THE DAMNED (2018)
(also producer)

Photo: Patsy Dunn

Joe Cornet is an accomplished filmmaker, having directed six feature films, with three of these projects showcasing his screenwriting talent as well. While he holds a special affinity for the Western genre, he has also delved into horror and other film styles. Now venturing into the realm of literature, *A Prayer for the Damned* marks his official debut book as a fiction author, with a promise of more novels to come.

Thank you for reading
A PRAYER FOR THE DAMNED
and Other Tales of the West

Please leave a review on your favorite
bookseller's website

For the latest updates on new books
from Henry Gray Publishing,
join our membership list at

www.HenryGrayPublishing.com

CHECK OUT OTHER GREAT READS FROM
HENRY GRAY PUBLISHING

THE LAST STAGE by Bruce Scivally

Dying in his small Los Angeles bungalow, with his Jewish wife, Josephine, whom he calls Sadie, at his side, famed lawman Wyatt Earp imagines an ending more befitting a man of his reputation: returning to his mining claims in a small desert town, tying up loose ends with Sadie, and – after he strikes gold – confronting a quartet of robbers in a showdown.

VEIL OF SEDUCTION by Emily Dinova

1922. Lorelei Alba, a fiercely independent and ambitious woman, is determined to break into the male-dominated world of investigative journalism by doing the unimaginable – infiltrating Morning Falls Asylum, the gothic hospital to which "troublesome" women are dispatched, never to be seen again. Once there, she meets the darkly handsome and enigmatic Doctor Roman Dreugue, who claims to have found the cure for insanity. But Lorelei's instincts tell her something is terribly wrong, even as her curiosity pulls her deeper into Roman's intimate and isolated world of intrigue.

THE UNDERSTUDY by Charlie Peters

"Tell your boss that I have one of his employees." With those words a kidnapping plot begins in the middle of a high-stakes corporate merger. But the kidnappers' plans don't unfold—they unravel.

"If you're thinking of committing the perfect crime, read Charlie Peters' elegant new thriller first. Find out just how many ways perfection can go wrong." – Dan Hearn, author of *Bad August*

THE DEVIL IN THE DIAMOND by Gregory Cioffi

World War II is coming to a violent close. As the Battle of Okinawa rages on, American soldiers seize Shuri Castle and find a single survivor: Yuujin Miyano. The U.S. private put in charge of watching the prisoner is Eugene Durante. Although enemies, the two men find they have a common multi-generational bond: baseball. Their grandfathers – one in Japan, one in America – bore witness to the magical birth of the game and helped shape it in the 1800s. When the war ends, the two men return to their homes to face a postwar world neither expected. Then both receive messages that change their lives forever: once more, the veterans will face off in a final dramatic clash.

For more info visit HenryGrayPublishing.com

THE MAN FROM BELIZE by Steven Kobrin

Life-saving heart surgeon Dr. Kent Stirling lives in paradise, dividing his time between two medical practices in the exotic Yucatan. Deeply in love with the woman of his dreams, he has everything a man could desire... until enemies from his secret past as a government hitman convene to eliminate him, including a death-dealing assassin known as the Viper.

SHELBY'S VACATION by Nancy Beverly

Fantasy. Sex. Despair. (Hey, what are vacations for?)

Shelby sets out from L.A. on a much-needed vacation to mend her heart from her latest unrequited crush. By happenstance, she ends up at a rustic mountain resort where she meets the manager, Carol, who has her own memories of the past inhibiting her ability to create a real relationship in the present. Their casual vacation encounter turns into something more profound than either of them bargained for, as each learns what holds them back from living and loving.

TOO MUCH IN THE SON by Charlie Peters

In Martinique, Leo Malone meets Taylor Hoffman, a young man who could be his identical twin. Whey they run afoul of a local gangster, Taylor is murdered and Leo assumes his identity to sneak safely out of the country and back to Los Angeles. But when Taylor's estranged parents meet Leo at the airport, mistaking him for their son, Leo's best-laid plans spiral out of control. Part Agatha Christie, part Elmore Leonard, with a dash of David Mamet and served with a Larry David chaser, *Too Much in the Son* examines the lies, intrigue and violence that make an unexpected family.

I CONFESS: DIARY OF AN AUSTRALIAN POPE by Melvyn Morrow

"When I became pope, almost the first word the Curia taught me was 'ricatto'—blackmail."   - *Pope John XXIV*

From acclaimed playwright Melvyn Morrow comes this engrossing tale of an Australian cardinal who has, through extraordinary circumstances, become pope. His personal diary reveals the inner workings of the Vatican and—when he begins enacting reforms and fears his tenur may be cut short—the centuries-old system in place to make sure that the status quo is maintained—at any cost.

THE ANTAGONIST by Emily Dinova

Dave Collins has a normal life - a loving wife, an angst-filled teenage stepdaughter, and a comfortable job. But one morning, he comes downstairs to find a yellow sticky-note on his refrigerator with a meticulously-drawn smiley face and the words, "You're special!"

Those two words set off a series of events that cause his entire life to implode, piece by piece, as if some unknown atagonist is purposefully ripping it apart. But who?

And more importantly — why?

YOU'LL FIND FUN WITH

PAPA ROCK'S HORROR MOVIES WORD SEARCH
by Rock Scivally and Jeffrey Breslauer

Sharpen your stakes—er, pencils—to solve these unique puzzles designed for anyone who loves classic horror films from the first Frankenstein film in 1910 to the giant bug movies of the 1950s.

If you grew up watching scary movies presented by a local horror host, or collected plastic model kits of monsters or read monster magazines, then this is the Word Search book for you!

PAPA ROCK'S SON OF HORROR MOVIES WORD SEARCH
by Rock Scivally and Jeffrey Breslauer

The 1960s. The 1970s. Two decades that encapsulated a shift in screen horror, from Dracula, Frankenstein, the Wolfman, and giant insects, to Blacula, Dr. Phibes, Regan, Damien, Carrie, a killer baby, and a rat named Ben. Pick up your pens, your pencils, or your blood-red highlighters and literally find all your horror film favorites from 1960 to 1979 within these pages. Happy Haunting!

PAPA ROCK'S ROMANCE MOVIES WORD SEARCH
by Rock Scivally and Jeffrey Breslauer

Here are Word Searches for 150 classic Romance movies made between 1921 and 1999, from the tragedy of *Camille* to the comedy of *Notting Hill,* with stops in-between for *Gone With the Wind, Casablanca, Roman Holiday, Breakfast at Tiffany's, The Way We Were, When Harry Met Sally, Jerry Maguire,* and *Titanic,* among many others. Just remember—if this book closes before you've finished working a puzzle, you'll regret it, maybe not today, maybe not tomorrow, but soon and for the rest of your life.

PAPA ROCK'S WESTERN MOVIES WORD SEARCH
by Rock Scivally and Jeffrey Breslauer

Westerns have been an enduring genre in American cinema from the very beginning. There have been serious Westerns, comedy Westerns, epic Westerns, and art-house Westerns. And you'll find examples of all of them in PAPA ROCK'S WESTERN MOVIES WORD SEARCH book. Within these pages are 150 Word Searches based on classic Western movies, including *The Searchers, Stagecoach, My Darling Clementine, Gunfight at the O.K. Corral, Rio Bravo, The Good, the Bad, and the Ugly, Dances With Wolves, Unforgiven,* and many more.

PAPA ROCK'S WORD SEARCH *BOOKS*

PAPA ROCK'S ANIMATED MUSICALS WORD SEARCH
by Rock Scivally and Jeffrey Breslauer

Animated movie musicals have been popular since the premiere of *Snow White and the Seven Dwarfs* in 1937. Since then, movie screens have seen musicals featuring animated animals and fantasy creatures, taking place in our own world and on imaginary worlds. Here you'll find 150 Word Search games with all your favorites, from Mickey Mouse to Charlie Brown to Strawberry Shortcake. Each puzzle relates to a specific film, where you can search for characters, actors, song titles, and dialogue phrases.

PAPA ROCK'S REVENGE OF HORROR MOVIES WORD SEARCH
by Rock Scivally and Jeffrey Breslauer

All work and no wordplay makes Papa Rock a dull boy... But there's nothing dull about this collection of Word Searches, each one featuring clues from a different horror film of the 1980s and '90s. Here are all your favorites – *The Shining, Friday the 13th, A Nightmare on Elm Street, The Fog, The Evil Dead, The Howling, Night of the Demons, Scanners, Creepshow*, and many more. So grab your pen… and work these puzzles until your head explodes!

PAPA ROCK'S WAR MOVIES WORD SEARCH
by Rock Scivally and Jeffrey Breslauer

Enjoy war movies? If so, then you'll enjoy this book of Word Searches where each one focuses on a particular war film, from silents such as *The Big Parade* and *Wings* to classics like *All Quiet on the Western Front, Sergeant York, Sands of Iwo Jima, The Bridge on the River Kwai, The Guns of Navarone, The Longest Day, The Great Escape, The Dirty Dozen, Where Eagles Dare, M*A*S*H, Patton, A Bridge Too Far, Apocalypse Now, Platoon, Full Metal Jacket, The Hunt for Red October, Saving Private Ryan*, and more.

PAPA ROCK'S SCI-FI MOVIES WORD SEARCH
by Rock Scivally and Jeffrey Breslauer

BALDLY GO WHERE NO WORD SEARCH BOOK HAS GONE BEFORE...

Go back or to the future with this book of Word Searches where each page focuses on a classic science-fiction movie, from 1902's *A Trip to the Moon* to *The Day the Earth Stood Still, Invasion of the Body Snatchers*, the *Planet of the Apes* series, *2001: A Space Odyssey, Soylent Green, Alien, Back to the Future*, the *Star Trek* and *Star Wars* movies, and more.

Join our mailing list to receive the latest news on upcoming titles!

9 781960 415295